D0192567

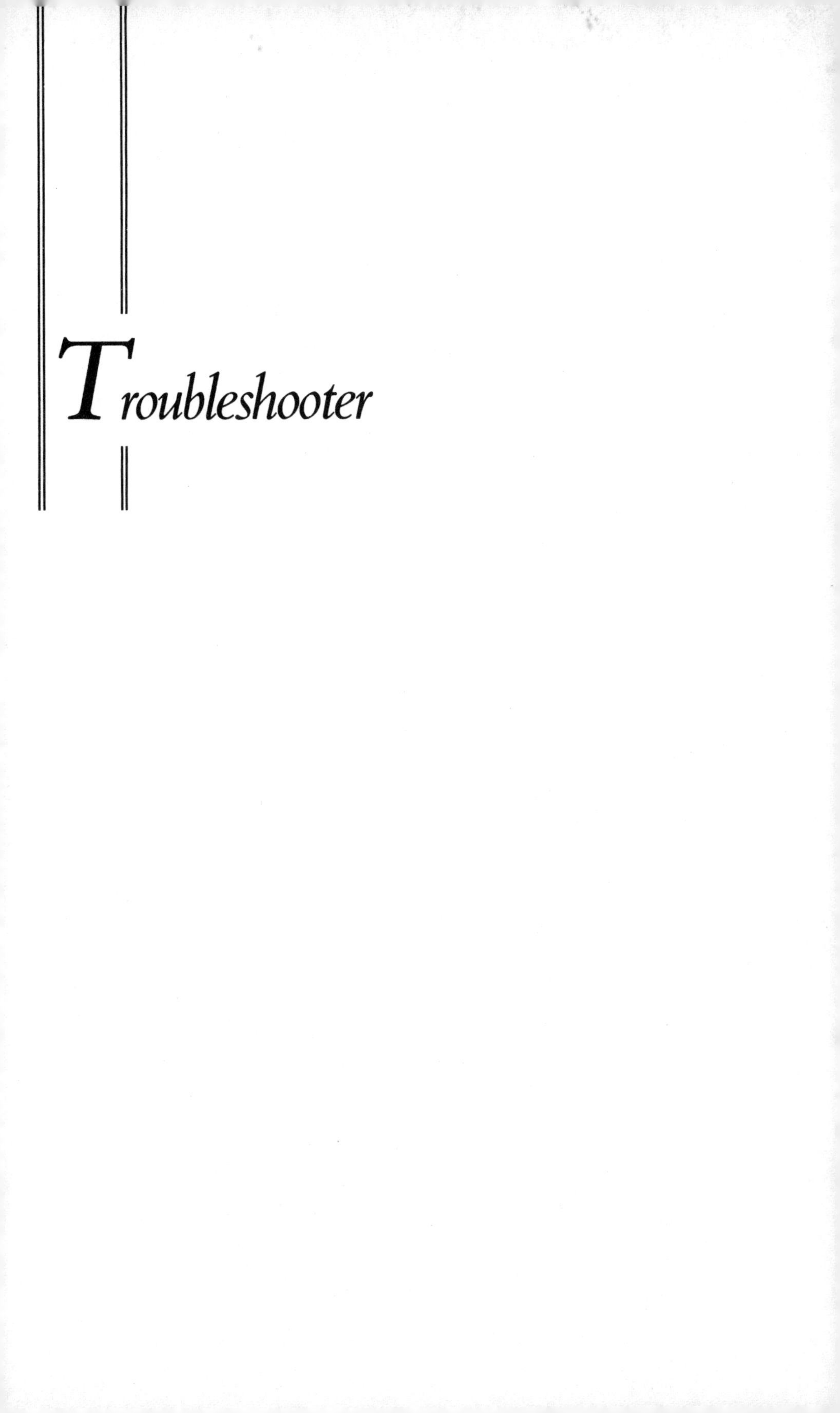

Troubleshooter

Troubleshooter

JOHN HARVEY-JONES
with ANTHEA MASEY

BBC Books

Authors' Acknowledgements

The authors would like to thank all those people, both inside and outside the organisations which are the subject of this book, for their help and patience in its preparation. Particular thanks must go to Robert Thirkell and Ann Laking, the producers of the BBC programmes on which this book is based.

ISBN 0 563 36009 7

Published by BBC Books
a division of BBC Enterprises Limited
Woodlands, 80 Wood Lane, London W12 0TT

Set in Bembo by Ace Filmsetting Ltd, Frome
Jacket printed by Belmont Press Ltd, Northampton
Printed and bound by Redwood Press Ltd, Melksham

Contents

Introduction

When it was first suggested that I should attempt a television series on companies with problems I must confess to having very considerable doubts, and to being far from convinced that I had anything special to bring to those companies. Despite having enjoyed over thirty years in industry and being credited with some success, I was uncomfortably aware of my own limitations. I had served both my apprenticeship and my time in the same company, albeit a company rightly renowned for the strength of its management expertise and ethos. Despite the fact that it was a very large company I had, of course, met and dealt with many small and medium-sized firms during my career as buyer and then salesman, and in addition I believed that I knew my craft. However, being able to apply these hard-won skills to totally unknown firms, situations and people, all the while under the scrutiny of the TV cameras, was a different game altogether. Even if I became so engrossed in the problems (which I was indeed destined to do), would the others appearing on 'the box' for the first time be able to forget this sufficiently in order to become engrossed in the actual task?

Indeed, were we likely to be invited in by anyone and, if

there were such companies around, how could we contact them and enlist their aid? We weren't offering much. Some unquantifiable help in the shape of advice – and a great deal of publicity, which could well be of the kill or cure variety. It is one thing to think you need help – but quite another to accept it. Defensive reactions come into play and it is all too easy to persuade oneself that one knows best after all.

I simply didn't believe that the programmes could be made 'for real'. The intrusive effect of the cameras, the knowledge that every reaction would be seen and analysed by thousands of strangers, as well as all the employees, customers, families and friends of everyone concerned – all seemed to militate against our accomplishing anything worthwhile.

Yet, despite all these doubts, the idea seemed to be one which had to be proved. I had inveighed long enough, both publicly and privately, at the low esteem in which industry and business are held in our country. I knew from first-hand experience how ignorant most people are of the realities of life in a factory. I was concerned that the brightest and best of our young people look on business in general, and manufacturing in particular, with a distaste and disbelief which lead all too many to turn their backs on such a life as a possible career. I have always believed that the future well-being of every person in the United Kingdom depends on improvements in manufacturing performance, for I see no other means by which we can pay our way in the world. Increasingly such success has to be achieved, not only against other British companies but against the industrial champions of Germany, America, Japan or Korea.

Failure to win this complex international battle will

inevitably and inexorably erode our standard of living, and with it our ability to pay for the infrastructure of a civilised society. Our ability to provide educational opportunities, health care, a research environment which would enable us to stay ahead, as well as roads, railways, a clean environment and so much else besides, rests on the straining back of our factories and businesses. If, therefore, the television programmes could inform people who had never even stepped into the world of business of the dramas and excitement of business life, that alone would make it worthwhile. If some of the firms we were to visit could also be helped to greater success, that would be a source of satisfaction – and an additional bonus for us all.

The advantages of doing the series may have been clear, but so were the risks. Until I actually got to the companies we couldn't tell whether I could do anything to help or not. I knew enough of business situations to know that the problems are seldom the ones they seem to be. Business problems are almost like the symptoms of a disease. The apparent ones are often the outward manifestations of deeper-seated management or personal issues, which must be worked on and cleared up before things can come right. For those involved in the day-to-day fight it is notoriously difficult to stand back and view what is happening dispassionately and analytically. Someone else sympathetic to the cause can quite often look at things in a different way and give a new perspective which can lead more easily to fundamental change.

It seems to me that this is particularly the case with smaller businesses. They have the advantage of speed of response, immediacy, and directness of contact with their people and their customers but, by definition, the chief executive is trying to be everything all at once. He cannot call, as the large company can, on specialists with personal experience of every arcane subject under the sun. Indeed, so overwhelmed are most chief executives by the heat and noise of the battle for survival and success that there is little opportunity for reflection on the wider issues involved.

In addition the job of the leader of a small firm is fraught with other difficulties and dangers of a different type to those of his counterpart in a large outfit. Both jobs tend to be lonely in so far as the chief executive cannot afford to show and share his doubts and worries. He feels that he must radiate confidence and calm, irrespective of his inner qualms. At least in large companies some of this can be shared with colleagues past and present, but the chief executive of the small outfit has no one to turn to, and misjudgements are even more exposed to his people. For the boss of the small industrial outfit the flip side of the immediacy of contact with his people and his customers is that it can seem as if he is working in a goldfish bowl where every action, mood, nuance or decision is known and judged instantly by everyone. It is, in naval terms, the difference between the captain of a battleship and the captain of a submarine, and the boss of a small outfit faces the same sort of demands on his personality and leadership.

I was certainly not interested in doing a propaganda job for industry in the sense of presenting a false picture, but I did hope that the programmes would help to show viewers why so many of us find the job so fascinating and so deeply rewarding. Business is not, as commonly believed, about numbers and endless computer calculations. It is about people and their interactions and dealings with others. In order to solve almost any business problem one has to persuade people to do something different, or do it in a different way. Moreover, the days when anyone would do anything (no matter how daft or how dull) for a pound or so, are long gone. People will do what they believe in and people will only change if they truly believe it is necessary to do so. Everyone prefers the safety of what they know to the uncertainty and possible excess of excitement in the unknown. And yet the greatest risk of all is not to change, for the world doesn't want the laggards, and the cut-throat competition from overseas has never even heard of the Marquess of Queensberry rules.

It is an illusion to hope that being small in some way shields one from these problems. Problems hit equally indiscriminately, but the small company has less time to effect the necessary changes. All small companies, even the best run ones, work on relatively small margins of cash flow and if troubles hit they have neither the resources nor the borrowing power of the bigger ones. Speed is essential – even though it is the enemy of caution, and small companies cannot afford the mistakes of the big.

My hope was that we could show these difficulties and conflicts in real situations, so that people who had not had these experiences would realise how testing they can be. Running a business calls for all the characteristics we admire in our folklore heroes, and yet it never occurs to us that they are to be found in the leaders of our small companies. Courage and compassion, vision and imagination, determination, persistence against adversity, creativity and wisdom are all called upon. Yet we persist in thinking of this occupation, which still employs one in five of our working population, as being dull, bureaucratic and for lesser mortals.

There was yet another aspect of the series which worried me. Inevitably we could only highlight a small part of the variety and diversity of the tasks which the executive must address. In all too many cases deciding what needs to be done is the easy part of the job. Actually making it happen is what counts, for the world of business is a hard task-master. You get no rewards for intentions. Only the accomplishment counts, and even then only if it puts you, even momentarily, ahead of the pack. Ideally I would have liked to be able to stay with the problems and persist until a way had been found to enforce the changes which seemed necessary, but this is what no exterior visitor can do. The home team has to deliver – and if it can't it must make way for someone else who can and will. The other motivation for me was the prospect of a sort of Johnsonian journey around a sample of British industry today. I knew and visited many of our largest companies, but it seemed likely that those who sought our help would be those with a turnover of less than £100 million a year. The chance of seeing some of them in rather more depth than a tour of their works and lunch with the board affords was a real lure. I love factories. A visit to a well-run works with modern equipment, and a well-motivated workforce, creating wealth before your eyes is, to me, both a thing of beauty and a source of real pleasure. A messy factory, disheartened and unhappy people, poor products and a feeling of defeat, produces just the opposite reaction and I long to roll up my sleeves and get stuck in. It is amazing how an efficient works shows in the demeanour and well-being of everyone around it. There are smiles and a sense of purpose, and work being done in a calm and methodical fashion. I am sure you can get a very good idea of the state of the company just by looking into the canteen.

There was very little doubt in my mind that I wanted to make the series if at all possible. I realised of course that the venture was quite a high-risk one from a personal standpoint. I could end up looking very foolish (to say nothing of arrogant) believing that I might be able to help people who, after all, live with their businesses twenty-four hours a day. However, it seemed to me that success, if it could be achieved, was so worthwhile that it far outweighed the price of failure. Even failure would show something to people who knew little of the business world, and it would certainly teach me a lot, for it is from one's failures that one learns, rather than from one's successes. Neither the producers nor I had any real idea of how to go about it. We knew that our time would be limited, both because of my availability and because of the costs involved. We were all determined to maintain the integrity of the process, to record it exactly as it happened and not seek to contrive situations for dramatic effect. We knew that we could not have a story line because our very first efforts showed us that the problems the firms thought they had were unlikely to be the problems which actually needed tackling. The difficulties for the producers were immense. We none of us knew when some casual remark would open up a path of questioning which would lead to the heart of the problem. But that is what it is really like. If the resolution of business problems could be carried out in a predetermined sequence, like a computer program, there would be no need for businessmen – and no role for sensitivity, intuition, experience or just plain common sense.

Business problems are the rather more interesting equivalent of being tossed a vast mixed and tangled ball of wool and trying to tease out the single end which unravels the lot. Wool at least is a relatively homogeneous product, whereas the businessman is trying to link numbers, people's beliefs, some facts, and a mass of related and unrelated evidence in order to find the pattern. Often, when the pattern does emerge, it looks so simple and so right that you wonder why such an obvious course of action has never occurred to you before. External events may still prove the simple solution wrong, inadequate or wrongly timed, but at least it has more chance of being carried through than the complicated one. I had, therefore, only moderate expectations that I would find executives who both accepted my advice and would then actually implement it. In the event I was to be surprised and delighted that some actions have resulted from my endcavours.

Once we were committed to the idea of the programmes the next step was to find the companies who believed they had problems of a size which could be dealt with in the relatively modest time we could make available. Despite my original pessimism we were amazed at the variety and range of industries and businesses that were interested in the idea. Indeed, our problem eventually became one of selection. I must emphasise that, just as this book is the product of four of us working together, so the programmes were very much a joint effort between myself and my friends and producers Robert Thirkell and Ann Laking. It would be almost impossible to disentangle the particular contribution that each of us was to make and almost all the decisions regarding the companies we should tackle were joint ones. Thereafter, however, we found ourselves involved in an unstoppable slide down a helter skelter – for each programme was a voyage of discovery in more than one area. The first dimension was that I had to get to know the executives and inspire in them sufficient trust for them to be prepared to discuss the realities of their problems openly. Although it helped that I was interested in their companies and genuinely wanted to help, the television cameras don't actually assist one to get to know people.

There were no 'set ups' and everything that happened was filmed or recorded – or both. Obviously, only a small part of the footage is shown in the films, but everything is shown as it happened. Given the reticent and withdrawn nature of many businessmen I was amazed at the way in which practically all of those I met threw themselves into the search for solutions. Our mutual interest in trying to reach the truth and decide what to do seemed to override the inhibitions I expected to encounter.

Another difficulty we had to deal with was that we could have no idea, until quite late in the process, which of the various possible solutions the company would wish to attempt to follow. There was no way around this. The accounts and some paper research before the visit could give a clue to some of the starting points, but quite often the real essence of the task would not emerge for some time. It was to be a true industrial 'whodunnit'. I feared that we might find the problems, and therefore the proffered solutions, repetitive and so uninteresting, and it is, of course, for viewers and readers to judge whether this is in fact the case. However, I was delighted at the variety of symptoms, solutions, challenges and opportunities we found in this small sample of a much-neglected and little-understood aspect of British industry. Some common themes (which I shall discuss in more detail in the last chapter) seemed to emerge during the series. These were of a very broad and generalist nature, far removed from the immediacy and singularity of the more obvious problems each of our companies was facing. This should not have surprised me, since management is the art of doing things through and with people. Every manager and every group of people is different, and so there are no stock solutions and no quick answers. Even when it appeared that there might be similarities, the way in which the problems presented themselves (and the range of possible actions) was always significantly different.

I found the programmes more taxing than I had expected. The combination of shortness of time, little research (except what the producers and I could do), and the necessity to do everything under the eye of the camera, put much greater stresses into the task than I had expected. This was particularly the case when I thought I could see clear and simple solutions and those concerned either couldn't or wouldn't accept them, even though they apparently accepted the logic of the argument. Under normal circumstances one would not accept such a position and would keep tackling the problems from different angles, until eventually some movement would occur, but in our case the caravan had to move on. However, I have stayed in touch with most of the companies and continue to follow their fortunes with a proprietorial concern and interest.

The whole process taught me a great deal. I learnt much about the complexities of TV production – even though I was no stranger to the medium – but even more about the magnitude of the tasks facing small and medium-sized businesses. Contrary to popular belief, most of the people I worked with are not highly rewarded. Very few earn anything like the sort of salaries which are being picked up in the City by people much younger and with far less impact on our national fortunes. They all work hard and are totally involved in the fortunes of the companies with which they work. Most are 'self-made', in the sense that they had not been trained in management skills, and in only one case was I dealing with the sort of professional hired management that I knew from ICI days. Most have significant personal financial involvement in their companies.

They are not, however, by the remotest stretch of the imagination, absentee landlords. The concerns of the executives are totally intertwined with their companies, their lives revolve around their businesses, and they are unstinting in their commitment and involvement with them.

We all owe a lot to these people. While it is the large companies which carry the brunt of our export earning potential on their backs, it is the small and medium-sized companies that provide both the import substitution and the bulk of the jobs. In some cases they do both, contributing more than their share towards the resolution of our balance of payments problems. It is on the vigour, imagination and professionalism of these small companies that much of our hopes for the future must lie. They need our understanding, support and help.

I hope very much that the series will have helped to show that business and industry is not about internal politicking and sharp practice. It is about decent men and women trying to earn a reasonable return by following the honourable calling which, during the industrial revolution, propelled our country from a tiny offshore island to a world power.

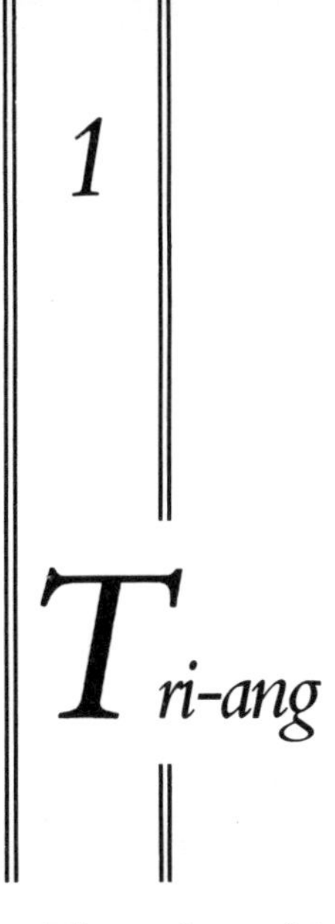

1 Tri-ang

There is nothing so powerful as our memories of childhood, which is why we are all so attached to the brand names which run like some continuous magical thread through so many happy birthdays and Christmases.

Parents and grandparents brought up in an era of Meccano sets, Hornby trains, Airfix plastic models and Dinky and Matchbox cars totally fail to understand the younger generation's passion for lurid plastic ponies with dayglo hair and see-through wings, and gory computer games more unpleasant than the worst video nasty.

Whenever one of these long-remembered names bites the dust, it is almost as if a little bit of ourselves dies, and along with it some sort of golden age of childhood, when mothers knew how to turn a collar and knit a Fair Isle V-neck and boys spent days building model Spitfires out of balsa wood and tissue paper.

It's all a lot of nostalgic nonsense but it does explain our almost obsessional fondness for our toy companies. And it probably also explains why the British toy industry was so totally unequipped psychologically to meet the electronic challenge of the 1970s and 1980s, and why so many of these famous names have disappeared from our toy shops over the last fifteen years.

Tri-ang is one of these evocative names. There can't be many people over the age of thirty who didn't scoot round the block on a Tri-ang scooter, or graze their knee falling off a Tri-ang tricycle. Tri-ang has had as many comebacks as a fading Hollywood star, and it came as a surprise to me to learn that the name still existed.

The rise and fall of Tri-ang, once the world's largest toymaker, its involvement with property developers and asset-strippers during the 1970s, reads like a business school case study charting the decline of Britain's manufacturing base.

The story of Tri-ang goes back to soon after the First World War when three Lines brothers, Walter, William and Arthur – three lines make a triangle, hence the name Tri-ang – started up in business. Toymaking ran in the family. Their father had a factory in north London which made wooden rocking horses, but his three sons branched out with a highly successful range of scooters and children's bicycles.

The partnership prospered throughout the 1920s and 1930s. The company known as Lines Brothers made the well-known Tri-ang scooters and tricycles, but there were also prams, mechanical toys and dolls' houses as well.

By the early 1920s Lines Brothers was strong enough to embark on an ambitious factory-building programme at Merton in south-west London, where it acquired an enormous 47-acre site. The company even took over Hamleys when the famous toy shop was threatened with closure caused by financial difficulties, and in 1933 Lines Brothers went public.

After the Second World War the company continued to

expand. The Pedigree soft-toy firm was established, factories were opened in Merthyr Tydfil in South Wales and in Belfast, and with the acquisition of Rovex in 1951, Lines Brothers started making electric train sets.

At the very height of the company's success in the 1960s, when it claimed to be the world's largest toymaker, there were forty factories scattered across the world and there was hardly an export market which the company hadn't penetrated.

But it was this hell-bent pursuit of growth which was to prove the company's undoing. In 1971, Lines Brothers shocked the nation when the company called in the receiver.

Tri-ang were rescued from oblivion by John Bentley, one of that notorious breed of early 1970s asset-strippers, not all of whom survived the coming secondary banking crisis. John Bentley's vehicle Barclay Securities sold off Lines Brothers' Merton site, in south-west London, and Tri-ang's entire production was moved to Merthyr Tydfil.

Tri-ang spent the next decade being rescued by a string of new owners. The Welsh Development Agency became involved, but no one had a bottomless pocket and just before Christmas 1982 Tri-ang was back again in the hands of the receiver. This time Sydney Orchant's Sharna Ware came to the rescue. With the help and support of the Welsh Development Agency, Sharna Ware bought Tri-ang from the receiver early in 1983.

I became involved at the end of 1987 at a time when Sydney Orchant had grand plans to relaunch Sharna Ware's range of wheeled toys and nursery furniture under the Tri-ang name and to invest an initial £1.5 million in modernising and re-equipping the factory.

It was just before Christmas, and the company was

getting ready to show a new range of products at the all-important Harrogate toy fair at the beginning of January. Sydney Orchant very much felt that the company was at a watershed, and he wanted my advice on how the company should proceed.

A former street trader, who sold elastic, combs, toilet paper and various other sundries, Sydney Orchant got into toymaking by accident. At the grand old age of sixteen Sydney had begun supplying other market traders from a warehouse off London's famous Petticoat Lane street market. His wholesaling business expanded to the point where he was approached by a Manchester businessman who wanted to start making plastic buckets and was looking for investors. Instead of investing in the buckets, Sydney took a stake in the company, and they named their new enterprise Sharna Ware, after Sydney's small daughter, Sharna, who was then just six.

It was another opportunistic approach, this time from an American businessman, which finally introduced Sydney to the toy market. The American was looking for someone to make a plastic sit-and-ride toy. It was while he was researching the toy market that Sydney Orchant ran into the name Tri-ang. At that time Tri-ang dominated the wheeled-toy market, and Sydney realised that if he was to succeed he had to challenge Tri-ang.

It is to Sydney's credit that he did, and won. By the end of 1982, when Tri-ang went into receivership, Sharna Ware had all but captured Tri-ang's market and Sydney found himself able to pick up one of the nation's best-loved brand names for next to nothing. Sydney continued making Tri-ang toys at Lines Brothers' Merthyr Tydfil factory for three years, but as it continued to make losses the factory was closed and in February 1986 production was transferred to Sharna Ware's Droylsden factory on the outskirts of Manchester.

The toy business was not Sharna Ware's only interest. There was also a chain of cash-and-carry stores, trading under the Orbro name. In the late 1970s these were providing the bulk of Sharna Ware's profits.

Sydney's interpretation of 'wholesale only' had always been generous, and the public were granted fairly easy access to the stores. This started operating against them when the big supermarket groups started competing on price with their big out-of-town superstores. Sharna Ware's profits reached a peak of just over £1.1 million in 1979 but by the mid-1980s, with the toy business taking more and more of Sydney's time, the stores started losing money.

Financial results for Tri-ang's holding company
(31 December year end)

	1979	**1980**	**1981**	**1982**	**1983**
Sales (£m)	15.1	15.9	17.3	20.7	24.7
Pre-tax profits (loss) (£000)	1008	383	548	687	806
	1984	**1985**	**1986**	**1987**	**1988**
Sales (£m)	27.5	30.6	25.7	9.3	11.1
Pre-tax profits (loss) (£000)	105	(295)	(492)	268	(314)

By the beginning of 1987, Sharna Ware had sold two of their stores and Sydney had decided to concentrate on the toy business.

The company now caught the eye of accountant Howard

Stanton, a former tax partner at accountants Stoy Hayward. He was on the look-out for what the City calls asset situations – publicly quoted companies whose shares are changing hands at well below their asset value. The attraction of companies like these lies in the tempting prospect of being able to buy assets cheap which can then be sold at a profit.

Sharna Ware fitted the bill, although in this case Howard Stanton was also interested in developing the toy business. In April 1987, Howard Stanton and J. O. Hambro Investments, part of the private company set up by Jocelyn Hambro and his sons Rupert, Richard and James, took a 29.9 per cent stake in Sharna Ware, investing £1 million in the company.

Howard Stanton, who held 10 per cent of the shares, became the new managing director, and it was announced that Sharna Ware was to be developed in four directions: financial, property, leisure and manufacturing. Sharna Ware's shares had a field day, more than doubling from 65p to 135p on the day the deal was announced and rising to a peak of more than 300p in August 1987.

Sydney Orchant remained chairman and was left in charge of the toy business, which his new partners agreed should be developed. Sharna Ware's first acquisition under the new regime was a toy pram maker, Telisport, which was bought the following July for £650,000.

Later that summer the company changed its name to Triangle Trust and in September the expected move into financial services came with the acquisition of Elliott Bayley, an independent insurance broker, for £2.7 million which was paid for in shares.

Sydney was chairman of Triangle Trust, but he appeared to have lost strategic control of what used to be his company. The decisions affecting the company's overall direction were now being taken by Howard Stanton and his partners in London, while Sydney continued to be based at the toy factory in Manchester.

It was the toy business which really interested me. It was hard to tell from reading the company's accounts and promotional literature whether the company was really exploiting the Tri-ang name. I got the feeling they weren't and I was very keen to find out if Tri-ang could once again become a world force in the toy industry.

There were several reasons why I wanted to see Tri-ang succeed. They are a manufacturing company. My first love is manufacturing, and I still believe it's desperately important for Britain to be good at it. Tri-ang is also a great name from my childhood and there aren't that many of those, so it would be nice to help put one of them back on the road to recovery.

The factory was not what I expected. At that time it was based in one of Manchester's majestic nineteenth-century cotton mills. Sadly the building had been neglected and clumsily converted, but it did have the advantage of space, some 200 000 square feet of it.

Sydney Orchant clearly loves the toy business and when we finally met I had no trouble believing him when he said how much he enjoyed bringing so much pleasure to small children.

I had wondered how much he was bothered by the fact that others were now responsible for deciding the company's overall direction. But far from feeling constrained, Sydney was clearly very optimistic about the future and the amount of money which might be available for re-equipping his toy factory. He was full of talk of using the Tri-ang brand name to build a world-class toy company capable of taking on the likes of Fisher Price, probably the world's biggest maker of toys for the under-fives, with the muscle of the giant US multinational, Quaker Oats, behind it.

There were a lot of question marks in my mind about the business. I wanted to know where the competition was coming from, and why Tri-ang had concentrated on a relatively small section of the toy market.

After a couple of hours with Sydney I began to get a feel for the strategy. There was a lot going on. There was a big advertising budget to launch a new baby walker and a new baby walking frame, and to relaunch the Tri-ang name, which was now going to be used to promote the Sharna Ware range of traditional wheeled toys. There was the purchase of pram-maker Telisport and a venture into garden furniture manufacturing, both aimed at reducing the company's reliance on the Christmas trade. And last but not least there was the planned first stage of a big capital reinvestment programme involving the expenditure of £1.5 million on three new plastic moulding machines.

Sharna Ware specialised in pedal cars, although the range also included an electric scale model Rolls-Royce, novelty bikes and tricycles and baby walkers. The common denominators were plastic, wheels and size – the toys were relatively large. According to Sydney it was the very bulkiness of the toys which kept the company afloat when most other British toy companies drowned in a flood of imports. The cost of transporting large items, such as pedal cars, half-way round the world didn't make sense even for the low-cost producers in the Far East. As a result companies like Sharna Ware didn't find their home market eroded by imports, although just recently they had noticed some imports from France which were selling at what looked like below-cost prices.

Having such a basically protected market does of course have its disadvantages. For a start, your business misses the honing edge of competition, a problem which at Sharna Ware was compounded by a predominant market share. I guessed they held some 70 per cent of the UK market for their sort of toy; a figure with which Sydney didn't disagree.

Over the years Sydney had experimented with other smaller toys for younger children, but had never been able to get the production costs right. He blamed this failure on his high factory overheads which made it difficult to compete with companies operating out of smaller, more compact factories. Having failed to solve this particular problem, Sydney decided on a different tack. At the time of my first visit, Sharna Ware was embarking on a new venture: making plastic garden furniture.

On one level the move made a lot of sense. Being big items, garden furniture makes good use of the factory's strengths, with the additional advantage of filling the factory's unused capacity in the first half of the year before the peak summer and autumn manufacturing period for the Christmas trade.

Not that the new venture was without risk. Diversification is a difficult trick to pull off and this was not a market with which Sydney was familiar. To be successful, Sydney needed volume in order to compete on price with the cheap European imports which dominate this market. I was somewhat reassured to learn he was embarking on this venture with a distributor who did know the market and who could handle the marketing.

Acquisitions to extend the product range were also planned. This was the attraction of Telisport, which made dolls' prams, buggies and baby walkers under the Telitoy brand name. The company was losing money when it was acquired in the summer of 1987, but Sydney was hopeful that an updated range of products would quickly boost sales and give Triangle Trust a useful foothold in the nursery market, where sales tend to hold fairly steady throughout the year.

Baby walkers, the kind of toy a toddler stands up and pushes, had always been a sizeable part of Sharna Ware's business. Recent scares about their safety had sent Sydney back to the drawing board. They had hired outside design consultants to come up with a completely new design which would have safety as its first consideration.

Baby walking trainers are different. These are walking frames designed to teach babies to walk. Baby trainers were not part of Sharna Ware's traditional market, but they were now selling one for the first time.

Sydney was pinning a lot of hopes on these two new children's products. He expected the baby walker to capture a big share of the market; he hoped the baby walking trainer would take him into new markets.

I now had a much clearer idea of the strategy Sydney had devised for Tri-ang, and I was ready to find out if the factory was capable of fulfilling his dreams for the company.

Frankly I was appalled. The mill itself, although antiquated, was absolutely fine and the factory was in an adjacent modern building; it was the manufacturing process which beggared belief. Here was a factory hoping to take on the best, most efficient toy companies in the world, yet the factory was chaotic and incompetently run. I couldn't see how Sydney expected to succeed in competition with top multinational companies when the flow of material through the plant was so erratic that his workforce was often kept waiting for batches of plastic and metal components. I guessed the plastic moulding machines were at least twenty years old, and could only be described as 'clapped out'.

In the circumstances, I was surprised to find the mainly

female workforce in such good spirits. They had plenty to complain about but on the whole seemed remarkably good-humoured. Left to their own devices, I am sure they could have organised the factory better themselves – they certainly deserved better management. I was also extremely concerned about safety. Many of the plastic components were trimmed by hand with a sharp knife, and accidents, some even requiring stitches, were frequent.

I ended my factory visit depressed and downhearted, so when I met Sydney's daughter, Sharna, and David Biggs, who were responsible for marketing, I was pleasantly surprised by the product range. It was attractive, well designed, it looked reasonable quality and appeared to offer value for money. But with such a large share of the wheeled-toy market already sewn up, I wanted to know how the sales team were intending to increase their sales.

As I saw it they had a problem. The number of children wasn't increasing, although I supposed each child was having more lavished on it, and there wasn't much scope for pushing up market share. Sharna and David told me the plan was to expand the product range. There were children's plastic furniture and garden slides which extended Tri-ang's range beyond wheeled toys. And they were expecting to expand the existing market with radical new designs such as their new baby walker, for which they forecast sales of 150 000–200 000 in the first year, and a new baby walking frame. And then of course there was the garden furniture.

Jonathan Ball, Tri-ang's design chief, confirmed the sales team's view that growth could only come from diversification into new product areas, which as I had already pointed out to Sydney was a high-risk strategy and bound to place the management under some considerable strain.

Jonathan concentrated mainly on the graphics and

colours aspects of the range. The new products were designed by outside firms of designers. I formed a very favourable impression of Jonathan, but it is a rare talent who can select and develop really world-beating products in an area as fast-moving and cut-throat as toys.

At the end of the day, I got together with Sydney and his top managers, including Ian Lever, the deputy managing director, the sales team, David Biggs and Sharna, and John Veasey, the company secretary, to discuss my initial impressions of the factory, the business and its future. What worried me was Sydney's ambitions for the firm. He was trying to do too many things at the same time – diversify the product range, relaunch the Tri-ang name, re-equip the factory – all of which carried their own risks. Obviously the company has to take some risks, otherwise it won't move forward, but I was absolutely convinced that it was important to phase in the changes.

Danger awaits any company which rushes at change. Existing management systems may not be adequate and tend to fall to pieces before more appropriate ones can be put in their place, and before anyone has time to draw breath the enterprise is facing a cash-flow crisis.

Managing change is difficult even with a strong management team and I had to tell them that quite frankly I didn't think they possessed the depth of management capable of even implementing moderate change. They were particularly weak in middle management.

The factory badly needed both a change of layout and new investment, and of the two I considered that change of layout should have top priority.

The company clearly needed new investment if it was to stay in manufacturing in the long term. Sydney had previously reassured me that the company's profitability had recently improved dramatically, to the point where it was projected to make an 8 per cent profit on sales. The company's previous record was much less impressive and on the basis of those historic figures any new investment would have been hard to justify financially. In addition to this, any decision on capital investment had to be taken at group level, and with Triangle Trust wanting to develop in areas other than toys, there was clearly going to be competition for funds. As I was seeing Howard Stanton the following week, I wanted to reserve judgement on this question of investment.

My other major concern was the market itself. With such a big share of the market for large wheeled toys already sewn up, David Biggs and Sharna were placing much of their hopes of growth on new products all of which in my opinion had several question marks hanging over them. The baby walker, although completely redesigned, and the baby walking trainer, are products about which mothers now have safety doubts, while the garden furniture, even with a distributor lined up, was a leap in the dark as far as Sydney was concerned.

If I had any preliminary conclusion it was that Sydney should as a matter of priority and some urgency get his management structure right before doing anything else. The existing management, especially the middle management, was not strong enough to cope with the amount of change Sydney was about to throw at them. He needed to make a number of appointments in middle management to strengthen the team, and I felt that he should only contemplate making changes once this crucial first step had been successfully achieved.

I then wanted to see the changes brought in gradually, as and when they could be efficiently implemented by management. Even a seemingly simple job like changing the layout of a factory actually requires careful planning and can place enormous strain on managers and workforce alike.

If there was any choice about where the money was to be spent, I suggested that the £500 000 which had been earmarked for advertising the relaunch of the Tri-ang name and the new products should be diverted to the factory modernisation programme. It was essential that the Tri-ang name went on the toys. In my view the name was already well enough known and the pay-off from an advertising campaign was unlikely to justify the expense.

I wanted to hold fire on my harsher judgements until I had had a chance to look at the figures more closely and had talked to Howard Stanton. Privately, though, my gut feeling about the business was that it had a real chance of being saved and it could grow, but that it faced some absolutely horrendous problems.

The factory was very old-fashioned. The flow of materials through it was terrible and production planning was just amateur. There was a 'not good enough' feeling about the place. It was good enough to just about survive, and it had been good enough to get them where they were. But with so little actual capital tied up in the business, this was not surprising. And in the end you can starve a business of capital for only so long. There will always come a time when the plant becomes uneconomic. It was my guess this time was fast approaching Tri-ang.

Many of the people who worked in the factory had been there for years and the management were lucky to have such a willing workforce. However, they seemed totally unaware of the level of worker dissatisfaction which was simmering just below the surface.

I concluded that unless Triangle Trust were determined to re-equip the factory, the business was likely to slowly but surely go down the drain. The factory was not efficient enough to fight on except by continually squeezing costs and there weren't that many more costs to squeeze.

I had resolved to tell Howard Stanton that the factory was worth saving. However, if it was to have a long-term future, it needed re-equipping, although he shouldn't risk that investment unless he was prepared to do something about substantially strengthening the management.

I also needed to know what Howard Stanton's intentions were towards the toy factory. If Tri-ang had had the misfortune to have fallen once again into the hands of an asset-stripper, I wanted to know. Perhaps he was content to run the factory down and get his money back by selling the buildings. If he intended keeping the factory, I wanted to know whether investing in it was a priority. I wanted to have his opinion of the factory and what it was capable of. I needed to check his perceptions against my own, and if they were different try and persuade him that mine were right.

But when I finally met him, a week after my visit to the Tri-ang factory, it wasn't really a question of having to persuade him of anything. Howard's background was finance and the City, and he openly admitted to having no direct experience of manufacturing. I found a receptive audience for my views, but I got the feeling that he had failed to get the measure of the toymaking business and was eagerly lapping up everything I could tell him.

It transpired that he had felt misled. When he had been negotiating to buy into the company, he had understood the factory was capable of increasing production by around a third. He now found this wasn't the case.

I told him that the quality of management was undoubtedly my principal concern. If Triangle Trust were going to put £1.5 million into the factory they needed to be sure that the toy business was being run by people who could really make that investment work and make it produce profits. Tri-ang's management were hoping to persuade the board to make this large investment in their factory, but no one had even bothered to make out a financial case for it. When I asked to see what kind of return Triangle Trust might expect, the Tri-ang management quite blithely said they hadn't yet worked it out.

Not surprisingly, Howard wanted to know if I would sell the toymaking operation. Any final decision on that had to be up to Triangle Trust, but I certainly wanted them to stay with the business. I pointed out that in spite of all the management problems the toy company had a lot of potential, particularly if it set about exploiting the Tri-ang name in a determined way.

Howard was equally attracted by the Tri-ang name and all it stands for: quality, reliability and good design. But he knew that if Triangle Trust decided to stay toymakers he would have to face some hard decisions. Should he continue to let the factory run down, or should he change the management and embark on a big investment programme?

By the time the meeting broke up, I thought we had both agreed the business was worth saving and that the factory could continue to make toys, and make toys profitably. We agreed to get together again, this time with Sydney, as soon as possible after Christmas.

The run-up to the Harrogate toy fair in January was always a tense time for Sydney. The company expects to see around 80 per cent of its customers at the fair, so a good toy fair with plenty of orders brings a successful year; a bad toy fair could mean unemployment at the Droylsden factory. The 1988 toy fair was particularly tense. This was the first time that many of the big buyers had seen the revolutionary new baby walker on which the company had pinned so many of its hopes. And in spite of my reservations, Sydney was still talking about getting enough orders to justify a big television advertising campaign to relaunch the Tri-ang brand name.

Sydney had clearly had a good fair and maybe it had gone to his head a little. Once again he was cherishing notions of becoming one of the world's leading toymakers, but how he expected to take on the likes of Mattel, Fisher Price and Tomy was never explained. In fact I was finding it increasingly difficult to get Sydney to look at the reality of his situation.

Orders from Harrogate were up 40 per cent on the previous year. Sales of the traditional lines, such as the pedal cars and the push-and-ride toys, were up 20 per cent, with the rest of the growth coming from the baby walker and other new products. It was certainly good news, except that Sydney had no idea of how he was going to get that level of production through his factory. 'Oh, we'll manage, we always do', was his rather nonchalant attitude.

Again the reality was rather different, as I pointed out. The scope for increasing production during the peak toy manufacturing period was actually very limited. The only way they could absorb a 40 per cent increase in the order book was to extend this peak period. But he had given no thought to what this would cost in terms of employing extra staff, and financing the extra work in progress and the higher levels of stock.

I continued to be even more convinced that the quality of management was the key to putting this toy company on the road to a profitable future. However, Sydney, who previously seemed quite receptive to the idea that he needed to do something to strengthen his middle management, was suddenly resisting any suggestion that he needed to hire new people. He didn't feel I had had time to properly assess all his managers. And for someone who in other areas could be so cavalier about costs, he wasn't relishing the prospect of putting another £100 000-plus on his payroll.

By this stage I was beginning to think the problem was partly Sydney Orchant himself. Sydney loves the toy industry, and I believe he loved that factory. This affection and enthusiasm for the industry was the most attractive thing about him, but equally I saw that his manner was quite often overbearing. His methods were essentially those of a proprietor of a small family business rather than a chairman of a public company.

I was also extremely concerned about the bizarre management structure which had developed since Howard Stanton and J. O. Hambro Investments had taken their stake. Roles and titles had been distributed in a manner which bore little relationship to people's actual function within the company. Howard Stanton was chief executive, but was based in London looking after strategy, and had almost nothing to do with the operation of the toy factory.

Sydney was chairman of Triangle Trust but didn't seem to have much to do with the planning of the company's overall direction. He was based at Droylsden and did little else but manage the toy factory.

These may seem like carping criticisms but, in my experience, having a transparent management structure which everyone throughout a company can understand can often be a very good indication of whether or not that company is thinking clearly.

A further symptom of the management's malaise was the poor relationship it enjoyed with its workforce. Sydney liked to pretend the factory was one big, happy family. After my visit to the factory I was far from certain this was anywhere near the truth.

Sydney liked to point to the fact that some of his mainly

female workers had been with the company for more than twenty years. But as the toy factory was a major local employer of female staff, this was hardly surprising. None the less many of the workers appeared genuinely fond of Sydney. Others clearly were frustrated by the lack of organisation which often left them short of components, and as this affected their work rate their bonus payments often suffered, leaving their pay packets short at the end of the week.

There was a works committee, and I asked several times during my visit to the factory to see someone from the committee, but somehow no one was ever forthcoming.

I had learned that the union was seeking recognition and had asked to ballot the workers on the issue. When I asked Sydney what he intended doing, he made it clear that he had run his factory for thirty years without a union, and he wasn't having one now. Why should he have a union, he operated an open-door policy, any worker who wanted to air a grievance was free to come and see him at any time. And anyway there was a works committee.

These were the excuses. However, the question of union recognition seemed to hit a very raw nerve with Sydney. Apparently the issue of union recognition had come up ten years previously and he had made an emotional appeal to the workforce, basically warning that he would throw in the towel if the union was recognised, and with the threat of losing their jobs hanging over them it is perhaps not surprising that the workforce chose to do without a union.

I didn't share Sydney's opinion that he had a happy, contented and competitively paid workforce. I certainly felt the shadow of discontent on the shopfloor and I was worried that unless Sydney faced up to the fact that he had a labour relations problem, he could find himself with a strike on his hands.

This marked the end of my involvement with Tri-ang. And my final conclusions? When I brought all my thoughts together I remained concerned for the future of the factory. I didn't think it stood a chance of surviving unless it was re-equipped. However, I didn't feel the current management was capable of managing the problems of expansion. Sydney's dominating personality pervaded the whole operation and middle management was weak and not sufficiently profit-oriented.

Sydney was not only a symptom of the problem, he was also totally indispensable. He was the only person who really understood the business, he knew the market place, he was well known in the trade, and he loved the toy industry with a passion, and as such I felt he had to stay in it at least while the factory was being modernised.

But Sydney was not the man to manage the brave new world, and he had to be manoeuvred into a position where new professional management could be brought in and given enough room to do their job without Sydney constantly looking over their shoulder. Tri-ang is intrinsically a good company. It has a strong market position and good products, and I for one would like to see it fly and re-establish the Tri-ang brand up there among the great names of the British toy industry.

As it turned out, events moved rather faster than even I had anticipated. Less than two months later, it emerged that Sydney Orchant's new partners had been dissatisfied with his style of management for quite some time. In the spring of 1988 Sydney was ousted. He resigned as chairman of Triangle Trust and left the toy company, his daughter Sharna having left at Christmas.

However, I was far from optimistic when I heard how

they intended to fill the vacuum created by Sydney's departure. John Veasey was promoted to managing director of the toy operation. While he was a competent company secretary and accountant, I was not sure he was managing director material.

Howard Stanton took over as chairman of Triangle Trust and the toy business. Again, Howard's lack of industrial experience worried me. I doubted if he was the right man to steer the toy business through a period of change.

My fears were not unfounded. In November 1988 Howard resigned from Triangle Trust after worse than expected first-half results from the toy operation. None the less, he had clearly taken to heart my major recommendation and during his time in charge of Tri-ang had started the job of strengthening the management. He made what turned out to be a highly significant appointment when he hired Mike Ganley to head up the marketing team. Mike Ganley is widely credited with having turned Waddington's ailing games division into the company's major money-spinner.

When Howard Stanton went, J. O. Hambro Investments was obviously worried about its investment. So much so that it sent in the heavyweights. Rupert Hambro stepped in as chairman, and his right-hand man David Harland took over as managing director. One of their first moves was to put Mike Ganley in charge of Tri-ang.

For the first time in many a long year, it seemed that Tri-ang was to get the professional management it deserved. Mike Ganley spent much of his first year recruiting an entirely new management team, including some of his colleagues from Waddington, and he now had a very strong marketing team.

I was sad they decided to pull out of manufacturing, but

I entirely understood why the decision was taken. The company now buys in plastic components for assembly and the enormous cost of re-equipping the factory has been avoided.

Mike Ganley describes Tri-ang as a marketing, distribution and assembly company. He decided not to get bogged down and diverted by the complexities of manufacturing. I was pleased to see that Tri-ang now had a manager who really had the bit between his teeth and who was marketing-led, rather than production-led.

Unfortunately, this is not my hoped-for happy ending. In August 1989, Tri-ang saw yet another change of direction when Triangle Trust took over the private interests of entrepreneurs, John Simpson and Conrad Williams, who then assumed management control of the now renamed Mayflower Corporation.

Mike Ganley hoped to persuade the new managers to back his ambitious plans for the expansion of Tri-ang, but they have decided that toymaking is not for them and in March 1990 Tri-ang was up for sale again.

I can only hope that Mike Ganley finds a buyer with the necessary will and the funds to save this once glorious brand, so that Tri-ang will be a name to conjure up happy memories in today's generation of children.

2

Copella Fruit Juices

More than fifty years ago a young Russian woman arrived in Suffolk from Palestine. She started to farm on the edge of the Dedham Vale, the countryside which inspired some of Constable's best-loved landscape paintings. Here she put down roots which have proved as enduring as the most blue-blooded of English families.

Devora Peake is a farmer, and the business she started more than half a century ago has changed, developed and survived to the point where it has become a sizeable family enterprise. Somewhere in this busy life Devora found time to bring up five children, three of whom now work with her in the family business.

The monument to Devora's achievement is Copella, the famous cloudy apple juice which has the familiar taste of Cox's Orange Pippins, hence the name C-O-Pella. So how did this endearing and hard-working woman, still with the vestiges of a middle European accent, come to invent what is after all a quintessentially English product?

The story goes back to the beginning of Devora's time in England, and I would make it required reading for every Minister of Agriculture, because the themes which have influenced the development of this family's business over the years – diversification, the development of the countryside for leisure, and organic farming – are the kinds of change which the government is now exhorting all farmers to look at.

Devora is a health food pioneer. She was living by the gospel of healthy eating long before there were health food shops on every high street and special health food sections in the supermarket. When she and her second husband Bill Peake turned the farm over to organic farming just after the war, people labelled them cranks. They ploughed a long and lonely furrow. As other farmers piled on the fertilisers and insecticides, the Peakes manured. As other farmers increased the amount they grew on an acre, the Peakes concentrated on growing their food naturally.

Today there is a growing interest in organic farming simply because it is beginning to make economic sense. We are growing more food than we need or can export, and we are all much more concerned about the avoidance of artificial effects on our food. Now people are prepared to pay more for food which is grown organically, farmers can afford to look at ways of growing less on each acre of land. Forty years ago these conditions didn't exist, and the Peakes undoubtedly paid an economic price for their beliefs.

But they were not discouraged, nor did they lack foresight. A big part of their income has always come from their apple orchards. In the late 1960s they saw that this part of their business would be under threat if and when Britain joined the Common Market, with imports flooding in from all over Europe. They decided to diversify. They bought a Swiss apple press and turned the apples they couldn't sell into apple juice. Copella was born. In their first year, 1969, they made just 20 000 bottles; now they make that amount in a day.

It was a brave move. It's hard to remember now, when the supermarket shelves are bulging with ever more mind-boggling blends of exotic fruits, that twenty years ago almost no one in this country was in the habit of drinking fruit juice – it was a weird transatlantic habit, enjoyed by people with more money than sense. You could find a few cans of frozen Florida orange juice buried at the back of the supermarket freezer cabinet, and if you were feeling particularly sophisticated you would buy a can of the stuff as a special treat for weekend breakfasts. But few people had or could afford to drink fruit juice daily.

It wasn't much later that the Peakes came to the sad conclusion that with their commitment to organic farming they were not getting an economic return from some of their poorer arable land. Looking for other uses for their unprofitable land, they hit upon the idea of opening a golf course. The Stoke-By-Nayland Golf Club opened for business in 1972, with one 18-hole golf course. At the time it was the only golf club for miles around, so in 1978 they opened a further 18 holes, and since then they have added a couple of squash courts and a snooker room, and membership has crept up to around 1400.

The need to find other economic uses for agricultural land to stop farmers producing food we can't eat or export but which we have to pay for through the Common Agricultural Policy was becoming a new and recurrent theme in government agricultural thinking throughout the late 1980s. But there is no doubt that the idea of turning the countryside into one enormous leisure park for jaded city folk, who would then clog up the landscape with their cars, crisp packets and lager tins, raises not a few farming hackles. What it doesn't alter is the fact that some farmers, the Peakes among them, have been developing leisure facilities and doing it well for the last twenty years.

And so the three arms of the Peake family business – apple, sheep and arable farming, fruit juices and the golf course – which, on the face of it, look an uneven mix, have in fact a very clear provenance, and have developed from the family's desire to keep one step ahead of the game while still clinging to their health food principles.

Bill Peake died just over ten years ago, and at the time of my visits Devora was running the business with three of her children and two sons-in-law. Devora is chairman and managing director. Most of the rest of the family are jacks-of-all-trades, most having responsibilities in several areas of the business. Devora's son by her first husband is Jonathan Loshak. A chemical engineer by training, he runs the golf club as well as looking after the company's computers; her eldest daughter by her second marriage, Susanna Rendall, is finance director, company secretary and personnel manager rolled into one; her husband Roger, a farmer, manages to combine running not only Copella's farms but also his own medium-sized fruit farm fifteen miles away, as well as being in charge of production. Devora's other daughter to join the family firm, music graduate Tamara, shares the job of marketing Copella fruit juices with her husband Stephen, a surveyor by training.

Over the last five years Copella has expanded the fruit juice side of its business. For years it was a specialist, small-scale producer of high-quality freshly pressed apple and apple juice blends. Copella was a brand you expected to see in health food shops and delicatessens, and as such shoppers were prepared to pay more than they would have paid for a supermarket brand.

But it wasn't long before the supermarkets became interested in stocking Copella. The booming fruit juice market meant that supermarket buyers were out searching for new ideas and new tastes to feed what was one of the fastest-growing areas of the grocery market. And Copella had something different to offer.

Most apple juice is clear and made from apple concentrate, much of which is imported from the Continent. Copella is a freshly squeezed apple juice. It actually looks as if it has seen an apple recently: it is the colour of apple flesh, it even has bits of apple floating in it. And what's more, it actually tastes of apples, English Cox's Orange Pippins in particular. This, coupled with the family's obvious belief in the superiority and health-giving properties of Copella, proved to be a winning combination, and from the mid-1980s most of the big national supermarkets were stocking the Copella brand at least in their larger stores.

But every successful product must have its imitators, and Copella is no exception. While the brand remained confined within the boundaries of the health food market it was safe, but as soon as it dared to put its head above the parapet, it became vulnerable to competition.

The supermarkets in particular wanted to have an own-brand English apple juice. For Copella, the temptation to supply this own-brand market proved too great. Marks & Spencer, which only sells its own label, liked it and wanted more. There were others too. Tesco and Safeway were both clamouring for an own-label product. The Peakes opted for a big expansion. They invested heavily in new plant to meet the growing demand both for their own Copella brand and for supermarket own label.

In theory expansion into own-label apple juice made a lot of sense. The Copella brand, with its high proportion of Cox's Orange Pippins, can only be made between October and April. The English apple juice the supermarkets want comes from a blend of English apples and can be made throughout the year. This gave the Peakes the chance to keep their pressing equipment busy throughout the year.

In practice expansion proved a mixed barrel of apples for Copella. They were producing more apple juice, certainly, but they found that most of their profits were going to pay the interest on the money they had borrowed from the bank to finance the new production.

They also had their share of bad luck. The hurricane which hit the southern half of Britain on the night of 16 October 1987, where it failed to uproot the whole tree, knocked most of the apple crop off the trees in the space of a few short hours. Apples now lay scattered and rotting on the ground: the Peakes lost 5000 apple trees that night and all their late-season apples. Nowadays, Copella tries to buy in most of its apples from nearby farms, and that year the price went through the roof.

So, after five years of booming sales, profits from the fruit juice operation turned into a loss in 1988. The Peakes did appreciate the risks they were taking when they opted for expansion and just how exposed they were to fluctuating raw material prices. They were able to renegotiate contracts with some of their big customers, but one of their largest, St Ivel, held them to contracts arranged well before the storm, which they were compelled to fulfil at a substantial loss.

The family are floundering, which is why they think they may benefit from some advice from outside their own close circle. They are spending a lot of management time

Financial results for Copella Fruit Juices
(30 April year end)

	1979(1)	1980(1)	1981 (1)	1983	1984 (2)
Sales (£000)	100	74	111	318	697
Pre-tax profits (loss) (£000)	3	(20)	(45)	14	50
	1985	**1986**	**1987**	**1988**	**1989**
Sales (£000)	1346	2011	2216	2270	2328
Pre-tax profits (loss) (£000)	86	109	18	(147)	45

(1) To 31 December
(2) 16 months

discussing the options facing them. They know they must make some decisions about the business, and there is a sense of urgency about their deliberations. Almost everyone agrees that the juice business will provide the key to the problem, but with everyone so close to the business, no one is coming up with any very coherent solutions.

They all know they are at a crossroads, and at one point Stephen says it feels a bit like getting stuck on Spaghetti Junction with no directions. There are so many possible roads down which to travel, but they need to unravel the spaghetti before they can be sure of finding the right route.

Tamara and Stephen, whose job it is to sell the apple juice, tend to look for marketing solutions. Copella has got where it is today with virtually no help from advertising.

To sell Copella, they rely on word of mouth, good press publicity – including the royal seal of approval, a picture of Prince Charles drinking Copella at a polo match – and the building of good relations with the retailers. To get more profit from the juice operation, they know they must sell more of their own Copella brand which makes money, rather than chase sales of own label to the big supermarkets, where profits are marginal. They are sure that a big advertising campaign for the Copella brand would work, but they can't afford to pay for it.

But there are other options. For years other companies have been knocking on Copella's door offering to take it over, inject capital, or take a stake in the company. The family are very happy working together and would prefer to stay independent, so they have been rejecting all advances. But now even Devora thinks they should be looking at the possibility of a partnership with another company who could put some muscle behind the Copella brand, although at the same time she is very concerned that the quality of the product shouldn't suffer in the process.

Arriving at Boxford, the village where Copella is the major employer, is a voyage down memory lane for me. I love the countryside around here. I lived in the area when I first joined the ICI board. The idea that Suffolk is flat and boring is not true of this corner of the county, where the landscape of gently rolling pastures still has the timeless quality which inspired Gainsborough and Constable.

I begin my visit with few preconceptions. I have looked at the figures, and apart from appreciating the financial problems of the apple juice operation, I feel I have only the sketchiest impression of what makes the company, its various component parts, and the family tick. However, no one who visits Copella could fail to be impressed by the warmth and generosity of the Peake family, and the obvious affection the members of the family have for each other.

Roger Rendall shows me round the apple packing and apple juice operation. Boxford (Suffolk) Farms, to give the fruit farm its full name, sells around 200 000 tons of apples a year, mainly to the big supermarkets. The apple orchards are the area where Devora has been forced to dilute her organic principles.

The trees in the orchards at Boxford do get sprayed, quite simply because there would be no business at all if they didn't. The supermarkets say most shoppers only buy apples if they are a certain size, colour and blemish free, and the buying power of the big chains is now so great that what they say goes. None the less there is a growing demand for organic fruit and vegetables, and some larger supermarkets are introducing organically grown fresh produce. The Peakes have recently planted 5 acres of organic apple orchard and these trees are producing apples for the retail market and Mrs Peake's apple juice, a new brand of organic apple juice.

Some of the women working in the packing plant have been with the company for thirty years. Boxford processes twenty-six varieties of apple, and grading these is a surprisingly skilled job. Not only do the packers have to watch out for blemishes and insect damage, but they have to know just how much colour is needed for any one of these varieties to be passed as grade 1 or 2.

Work in the packing house is obviously seasonal, but many of the women work somewhere in the business all year round. When apple packing is over, they can sort apples for the juice plant, or work in the orchards pruning and tying back the trees.

Copella is made from a blend of apples, predominantly Cox's Orange Pippin. I had originally thought that Cox's were the only apples used, but apparently a juice made only from Cox's would be too sweet even for our national sweet tooth. Although the juice business was started as a way of using the apples the farm couldn't sell, the business has expanded to such an extent that today the farm only supplies 5 per cent of its needs. The rest of the apples are bought from surrounding Suffolk farmers.

The nature of Copella makes it an inherently costly juice to manufacture, and the family, even in the face of financial problems, have never been prepared to compromise their standards. Copella is a freshly squeezed juice, with no added water, sugar or preservatives. To get that distinctive, clean taste, the apples arrive in small bins to avoid being damaged, they aren't loaded in bulk, they are washed, hand-graded and washed again. Only then is the juice pressed and flash pasteurised. Not for Copella giant hoppers indiscriminately filled with any old apples which feed directly into the juicer.

Most processors of fresh fruit and vegetables come up against the problem of the seasons. Modern farming methods have extended the cropping seasons of many varieties, but when working with a traditional apple like Cox's you are stuck with the characteristics of that particular variety. The season of the Cox's apple is very short, and the apple doesn't keep particularly well. The main production season is between October and April, during which time a year's supply of Copella is made. Not being able to turn the production tap on and off during the summer is an obvious disadvantage.

The weather is the major factor affecting the demand for all soft drinks, and Copella is in the difficult position of having to best-guess next summer's demand in the depths of winter. According to Roger Rendall, they have run out of Copella only once in fifteen years, and then just for a week. They would have run out during the long, hot summer of 1989, if they hadn't been able to start the new season's production almost a month early, at the beginning of September.

The seasonal factor places an additional financial burden on the company, which is forced to finance and store excessively large stocks for much of the year. At the end of the company's financial year at the end of April the juice operation is usually shown as carrying stocks of around £750 000.

The plant and equipment is shut down for a week during the summer for full cleaning and maintenance. The rest of the time, routine maintenance is carried out as and when it can be fitted in, mainly over weekends. This can lead to a loss of production at peak periods. It's an area where the then production manager, Martin Bartlett, would like to see some more investment. He has calculated that new equipment, costing around £120 000, could increase juice production by 10 per cent.

I am surprised to find that the company does its own distribution, and owns a small fleet of lorries and vans. This is quite an unusual arrangement and I am convinced it is an additional expense for the company, which is unlikely to be running its lorries and vans at the kind of capacity a commercial haulage firm would consider economic. Food companies much larger than Copella find it cheaper to use commercial haulage firms rather than carry out their own distribution. The family claim they are far from convinced that they could get the kind of service they need if they didn't do it themselves. At the moment a supermarket order for Copella received at 5 o'clock in the evening is in their customer's warehouse by 6 o'clock the next morning.

I now move on to meet Devora's daughter, Tamara Unwin, and her husband Stephen. It was Tamara and Stephen who went out and chased the business, got the Copella brand on to the supermarket shelves and supplied the supermarkets when they started clamouring for an own-brand English apple juice. The juice business has been sales driven. Tamara and Stephen won the contracts; investment in new production followed. I had learned from people in the industry that Tamara and Stephen were not only liked, but their work with the Copella brand was highly respected. I subsequently learned that some of the companies which came to court Copella were as interested in Tamara and Stephen's energy and drive as they were in the actual production facility at Boxford.

Tamara and Stephen are clearly still very ambitious for the product, although they recognise that the business will have to change. Tamara in particular feels that the family has maintained the brand leadership in freshly pressed apple juice and is not ready to give up yet. She believes the brand could go further if only they could have some extra help with sales and marketing.

I am still feeling my way at Copella, but my initial reaction is that simply increasing sales won't solve many of the structural problems which face the business. Pushing extra volume through existing production facilities would normally increase the profitability of the entire operation. But in the case of Copella, where the product can only be made during a short season and has to be stored ahead of the busy sales period, increasing production simply brings with it additional financing costs.

I don't feel the Copella brand is sufficiently differentiated from its rivals. I have been drinking Copella out of bottles for years, but only when I came to Boxford did I realise that the product was significantly different from other apple juices, even other freshly pressed apple juices. Where on the label do I learn that there is no added water, or sugar, and that, most importantly, the apples used are predominantly Cox's Orange Pippins, possibly the best-loved of all English apples? Here is a product which seems afraid to proclaim its superiority – I have to search the label to find the all-important information about the apple variety.

I would be opposed to putting a lot of the company's own money behind the brand with a massive advertising campaign. I would prefer to see the company try to reposition the Copella brand higher up the market, carving out a new specialist niche for itself, which consumers would recognise and would be prepared to pay for. I do believe, and what's more the entire family believes, they have the best brand on the market; what I feel they now need to do is make sure the shoppers know it too.

Neither Tamara nor Stephen is convinced the brand could stand a big increase in price. Stephen points out that Holland & Barrett are at that time selling cartons of Copella at £1.09 each, double the price of supermarket own-label apple juice.

They claim that Copella is already made to stand apart. It is sold in cartons only in health food shops like Holland & Barrett,where shoppers know the product and know they are getting a premium apple juice. In supermarkets, however, Copella is sold only in 70-centilitre bottles. They use bottles rather than cartons for two reasons: to give the brand a luxury image, and to make it more difficult for price comparisons to be made with the cheaper carton products. At the moment the Copella price is moved up once a year and although Stephen is nervous about trying to shift the price up by a significant amount, he concedes that no sales resistance to price increases has ever been noticed, and that perhaps they could try moving the price twice a year.

Tamara is not at all keen on testing the price elasticity of the Copella brand without the support of some third party. Selling a stake in your company is always an option for a family business which has reached the point where it can no longer fund expansion from its own resources, and it becomes clear that this is an option which the family is now seriously considering.

However, the particular circumstances of this family business make me reluctant to recommend this particular route. The family, and in particular Devora, care passionately about Copella the drink, its quality and its health-giving properties. Surrendering control to a third party, whatever initially sympathetic noises they make, will inevitably lead to the product being compromised in some way which this family would find deeply distressing.

I am tentatively moving towards the view that Copella is a premium brand which is being sold too cheaply, with the result that no one really knows the true size of the market. The company could try to cut the overheads but, without drastically changing the product, savings will be hard to find. Companies produce premium brands because they earn a high margin or percentage profit on sales.

Copella has found itself caught with a high-cost, premium brand which in profit terms is just not performing as it should. Of course, if it does try to push the public's perception of the brand up-market, it may end up earning a healthy margin, but by the same token may find it is servicing a much smaller market.

Tamara and Stephen ask me what I think about just selling the name. If they are washing their hands of the brand, they might as well sell the whole business. Selling just the brand leaves them with the problem of what to do with their juice pressing and packaging plant. Brand-only deals like these generally prevent the previous owners from setting up in opposition to the brand they have just sold, at least for a number of years.

I now drive over to see Jonathan Loshak who has been running the golf course in the nearby village of Stoke-By-Nayland for the last sixteen years. He is clearly very attached to the club and what, if he weren't a more sensitive man, he would probably call 'his golfers'. But he is also very worn down and exhausted by the long hours that the job involves.

Since opening in 1972, the club has doubled its size by opening a second 18-hole course in 1978. The clubhouse has been extended, snooker introduced, two squash courts built, and the bar and restaurant facilities are always being improved. There are some 1400 playing members and the number is still growing.

As a business, golf clubs are strong on assets, but tend to show a relatively low return on investment. Stoke-By-Nayland Golf Club makes a profit, but as yet there isn't enough money to employ a full-time manager to ease Jonathan's workload.

Jonathan has been very successful at pulling in the membership, but one of the problems of running a golf course is that the facilities are used very unevenly, with heaviest use at the weekend. Golf clubs make most of their money in the bar and restaurant, so the more people they can get through the clubhouse, the better they will do. Jonathan devotes much management time to addressing this problem, pulling in bookings from societies and businesses to fill the club during the slack periods in the week. The club has now built up quite a reputation for arranging this sort of activity, and some groups return year after year.

I think the golf club has tremendous potential for expansion. I would like to see it develop along the lines of some successful country clubs that I have seen near my home in Herefordshire. I am convinced the country club is a concept which is only now coming into its own, and will be a major area of expansion over the next twenty years. Busy, aspirational families don't just want to relax at the weekend, they want activities they can do together and which they feel are doing them some good. The idea of being able to drive to a facility, out in some lovely countryside, where in one location the family can find golf, country walks, swimming, squash, a gym, as well as somewhere pleasant to eat and drink, is obviously very attractive.

I am surprised to find that Jonathan is strongly opposed to the country club idea. He feels that golfers come to the club for no other reason than to get away from their families for a few hours' peace and quiet, and that they would resent having to share even an extended facility with hordes of children. I think he is failing to recognise how family life is changing. While his view may have been true of an older generation, these days younger men are much more involved with their children. The idea that dad slopes off to the golf course on a Sunday morning while mum slaves over the Sunday lunch is a stereotype from the 1950s. Today it seems just as likely that golf clubs are failing to appeal to younger players because there is nothing for the rest of the family to do.

Susanna Rendall, finance director, company secretary and personnel manager, picks me up from the golf club and drives me round the last corner of the Peake family empire: the farm. On the way we see the five reservoirs that Devora built on the farm with the help of government grants. The Peakes haven't found a way of exploiting the reservoirs as a leisure facility, because they are surrounded by the golf courses. So far they have remained purely functional, although with rainfall in this corner of Suffolk some of the lowest anywhere in Britain, having a private water supply proved to be an almost priceless asset during the long hot summer of 1976 and again in the summer of 1989.

At the end of the day I get together with all the family to give them my first impressions. I've had an enormously enjoyable day, and feel very lucky to have been at least temporarily a member of this remarkable family.

Family businesses, where everyone enjoys working together and where there is a great deal of mutual respect for each individual's contribution, as with the Peake family, can suffer from a lack of frankness. It can sometimes happen that the bonds of love and respect are so strong that individuals are constrained from saying what they really feel, for fear of treading on someone else's cherished aspirations.

On the other hand, most successful businesses build in mechanisms which allow managers to be frank and open, in both praise and criticism, and in fact I am absolutely certain that keeping an open and uncluttered mind is one of the most valuable attributes of a successful manager.

The family are already considering a number of propositions from third parties, but I am concerned that before they rush into anything they must be entirely honest with each other about what they want to do as individuals. They are not just talking about a family business, they are talking about how six energetic and enthusiastic people will be spending the rest of their lives.

At the most fundamental level the family have achieved a great deal: they have built a business with a very strong asset base. But what they haven't been able to do is get those assets to the stage where they are earning a decent return. The family may be wealthy on paper, but in terms of actual cash in the bank no one could ever accuse them of milking their assets dry.

This imbalance between assets and income could probably have been sustained for longer, had it not been for the hurricane which sent apple prices soaring and cash flow forecasts into free fall. The family fully understand now that this imbalance must be righted, and that assets must be sold. Now they must decide which bits of the business are worth staying with and which can be disposed of. I get the feeling the family agrees with me that the apple pressing operation holds the key to their particular conundrum.

But how? At this stage I really want to go away, talk to some other people and work on the figures before I make my final judgement. The family do not let me off that easily. I end up telling them they would be much better getting out of the apple pressing operation entirely. There is a slight frisson of horror when they think I mean closing the plant. In fact I don't want the plant mothballed. I am sure that plenty of companies would want to buy the operation, and for a sizeable sum of money. And as I have already said to Tamara and Stephen, I think psychologically it is better to sell a business outright rather than risk a partnership with someone who may have very different ideas on how to run it.

Before making any final recommendation, I need to do some more research. I want to test my reaction to the apple juice operation and the Copella brand on an expert. As a non-executive director of Grand Metropolitan, I have watched the development of Aqua Libra, a new up-market soft drink which the company has successfully established over the last couple of years. I want to know if there is any way of giving the Copella brand a stronger, more luxury image.

Chris Burton has spent most of his working life in the fruit juice business and, as a director of a leading fruit juice importer, is in an ideal position to monitor trends.

According to him we British have been acquiring the fruit juice habit very fast. Only twelve years ago we were drinking just a litre per year per person; now that figure has risen to around 17 litres a year. Orange is still the most popular juice, with apple juice in second place. And of course it's big business, with orange juice turned into concentrate in high-tech factories in South America and then carted around the world in giant tankers. There is even an orange juice futures market.

Orange juice is now just as much a commodity as sugar or cocoa, and the same thing has happened to apple juice. The introduction of cloudy English apple juice by a handful of specialist producers created a niche market, but this was quickly invaded by the supermarkets, who introduced their own brands, and now this too is fast becoming a commodity with prices constantly being driven down by the buying power of the supermarkets.

Chris Burton does think Copella's special ingredient – Cox's Orange Pippins – is a sufficiently strong selling point to put it in a category where it could command a significantly higher price. The fact that Copella is sold mainly in bottles is obviously a help, as this avoids comparison with cheaper products sold in cartons. But he feels that there is nothing about the current design of the bottle and label to make shoppers believe they are buying something really special.

The new Mrs Peake's organic apple juice is obviously a useful addition to the Copella range; but if the company relies on apples supplied from its own farms it will have problems if it wants to make the new juice in any volume because as yet it has only very limited supplies of apples. But with the current scare about the presence of Alar in apple juice – used to produce regular-shaped fruit – any company selling an organic apple juice guaranteed Alar-free could charge almost what it liked.

Chris Burton is convinced that the trend towards more healthy eating is the key to the successful development of products for the 1990s. But as this trend has already been recognised, it is not necessarily an instant road to success. He doesn't feel organic products will automatically succeed, but he does say companies ignore the trend at their peril.

Copella can take some consolation from the fact that it is not alone in finding the fruit juice market tough. The buying power of the big supermarkets and the dominance of own-label brands, which occurs nowhere else in Europe, has driven down margins for all fruit juice processors.

From what Chris Burton says it seems to me that here is an industry which is due for a big shakeout and that eventually capacity will be taken out, with companies going bust or being taken over.

But whatever happens the industry will be saddled with some inherent marketing problems. The successful companies will be those who develop genuinely new products which create their own niche markets and can therefore command a price which won't automatically be compared with the cheapest of fruit juice in a supermarket long-life carton. But although this can give companies an advantage for a while, fruit juice products are generally very easy to imitate, and it is never long before copycat products start driving down the price, and with it the processor's profit margin.

Chris Burton agrees that Copella brand could stand a price increase but warns against making this without substantial changes to the packaging, such as a touch of gold champagne-type paper round the tops of the bottles, to reassure shoppers that this is something really special.

Now that I have confirmed most of my initial fears about the structural problems of Copella's fruit juice operation, I feel more confident about making some recommendations to the Peake family.

I think I shall have quite a few problems getting the family to accept that there really is a fundamental problem with what they rightly consider the jewel in their crown, and that they have now pushed their fruit juice operation just about as far as it can go. But this is a family business, and realistically I understand that for the Peakes the welfare of each member of the family is just as important as the pounds, shillings and pence on the bottom line.

For Devora, Copella is like her sixth child, so selling the business would be like sending a member of her family to live in an orphanage. But whatever happens Devora is going to find it difficult to change. She won't like the idea of having to charge people more for Copella. Her belief in the brand and its health-giving properties would make her resist any idea of making it so expensive that only a few people could afford it. And then there is the purely practical problem of what would happen to the two family farmhouses, situated at the heart of the juice operation, if the business was sold.

I am sure that Tamara and Stephen would also have great difficulty in letting go of Copella. It is largely due to their efforts that Copella has grown so rapidly over the last five or six years, and because they are so close to it they remain convinced the brand has a lot more growth in it. Apart from anything else, cutting the ties with Copella would deprive them of the job they know and love. Emotionally it would be a tremendous wrench, but it's an option I think they should try and look at objectively.

It is a confusing time for all the family. Up until recently they have been able to repel all outside offers of help. Now they know they must change. Various proposals have been put to them by other companies in the food and drinks business, but they have stalled any final decision until they have heard what I have to say.

What I am doing here, in a small way, is in many respects similar to what I was doing all the time at ICI. To be successful in business you don't have to lack warmth, and you are certainly allowed to become attached to your business. In fact you probably can't inculcate into your workforce the necessary attention to detail, unless you do become attached.

But still there has to be part of you which remains ever analytical and ever critical. Businesses can't stay still, they must initiate, grow, change and adapt if they are to survive. Businesses don't have to be like people, they don't have to grow, mature, decline and die, although sadly many do. And this is particularly true of family businesses. The good manager's steely eye must forever be making adjustments about which parts of a business must be pushing forward, where investment is likely to show the best return, and which bits should now be discarded.

It is this good manager's steely eye which I try to bring to Copella. But when implementation is not up to me, my really difficult job is actually getting people to stand back from the day-to-day involvement with their enterprise so they can really see it for what it is.

I am convinced that the best way to promote the Peake family's fortune is to concentrate on the golf club, and build it into one of the best country club facilities in East Anglia. This requires investment, and much of the money for this can be raised by selling the fruit juice operation before it is too late and no one wants to buy it. The farm should be retained. It more or less washes its face at the moment and, even if it sticks to its organic principles, I don't see why it shouldn't continue to do so. But the main economic reason for its retention is as a land bank from which the leisure development can draw as it expands.

It's now a month later. I am back at Boxford, and I am sitting in Devora's garden with Devora, Tamara, Susanna, Stephen, Roger and Jonathan.

I feel that unless I can make the family understand the very real structural problem they are facing in their apple juice operation I am lost, and I won't get the chance to really hammer home the message of what an exciting opportunity they now have to develop their leisure business.

We talk about the bulk juice business. This keeps the plant busy at those times of the year when Copella can't be made and, if costs are to be contained, the Peakes have no option but to continue supplying the big supermarket groups. However, they must expect conditions at this end of the market to get tougher and tougher. Just pushing more bulk juice through the plant is not going to be any solution to their problems.

They can reduce costs by being less fastidious in the way they produce their juice, although emotionally I don't believe they could do this. They could also increase the yield with the help of some extra investment. Beyond this, however, there is not much scope for further cost reductions. Costs are already low: the family don't pay themselves very much, spend almost nothing on marketing, and operate in a low-cost area, with an admirably flexible workforce who work on the farm, in the orchards or packing fruit, when they aren't working in the juice plant.

With Copella, they have the chance to differentiate the brand still further. The strategy here must be to redesign the bottle, making it look the champagne of apple juices, and then push up the price by possibly as much as 40 per cent, probably in stages. The volume would fall, but the margin would rise substantially, because lower volume would bring with it lower financing costs, with less juice having to be stored. I am also convinced they should push Mrs Peake's organic apple juice, although they should be clear that in this area, as with Copella, they won't have the market to themselves for very long.

I don't think they need to embark on a big new marketing push. I have been tremendously impressed by the reputation of the brand in the marketplace. The brand might be helped if, in those supermarkets which have specialist health food sections, it is moved out of the soft drinks section, to identify it more closely with higher-priced health foods. This does mean effectively bringing the product right back to where it started in health food shops, but I am not sure Copella can command a premium price if they try to differentiate the product in the drinks section.

Copella also sells a range of apple juices blended with other ingredients: there are strawberry, blackcurrant, morello cherry, pear, and even a carrot blend. No one in the family is making exaggerated claims for these products, but from a marketing point of view they inspire confidence in the company. In reality, Copella is a one-product company, but being able to offer a range of products, at least it doesn't look that way. I don't feel any of these apple juice add-ons are sufficiently original, to create a new niche market. They are nice to have but basically peripheral to the main problems of the business.

The Peakes have also discussed launching a chilled product. Freshly squeezed juices are sold from the chill cabinet and are packaged in either plastic bottles or short-life cartons that have a totally different appearance to long-life cartons. From Copella's point of view the possibility of selling a chilled apple juice presents certain problems. Because the juice has a relatively short production period, and chilled juices can't be stored, distribution would be restricted to six months in each year, and most big supermarkets would be unhappy about stocking a product on that basis.

I don't think anyone can be in any doubt that my prognosis for Copella's apple juice business is basically quite gloomy. Having, I hope, made this very clear, I now want to try and persuade the family to look at their business as a professional manager would. I know they love their product. They have lived with it for twenty years and facing up to the possibility of no longer being involved with it is very difficult.

But in a curious way I feel responsible for this family's economic well-being. I want them to be in a position where they are earning a decent reward for all their hard work. At the moment they work all the hours that God gives, for precious little reward, and in the long run that isn't good for anyone. Eventually it will lead to family resentments and tensions, and in many ways I am absolutely astonished that the atmosphere is still so good-natured in spite of all the difficulties.

I want to make them see that what I am proposing, although quite a radical solution, is really the best way forward for the family, and holds out the best hope for developing a profitable, growing business capable of being passed on to the next generation of Peakes, if that is what they want.

I think they stand the best chance of success if they sell the fruit juice operation and sever all connections with that part of their business. The money raised can then be used to repay borrowings and restructure the rest of the business. A plan for further investment in the golf club can then be evolved which will expand the business by taking it into other leisure areas; the farm would be kept ticking over as a land bank for the future development of the leisure business.

I am also convinced that if they do decide to sell the business outright, they mustn't just sell it to the first-comer. They must get proper professional advice in order to avoid many of the potential pitfalls in what on the face of it seems the relatively straightforward job of selling a business.

The only person who doesn't feel a deep emotional attachment to Copella is Jonathan, and I had clearly underestimated everyone else's attachment to the fruit juice operation. They all want to know if there is any way for them to stay involved with Copella. Of course, they can: it's up to them. But once again I warn against half-way houses. If they sell control of their company but stay involved they are no longer proud, independent people; they become hired hacks. It becomes somebody else's business, someone else is calling the shots, someone else is running the brand and they may have different ideas, different priorities.

They would also get less money for the business, and would still be spending their management time on Copella. The advantage of a clean break is that it would mean more money and more management time could be devoted to developing the leisure activities.

In spite of everything I have said, I fail to convince Devora that the problem is rather more serious than just spending money on promoting the brand, and that far from being a solution, simply pushing extra volume through the plant could actually make things worse.

It is only now that Devora reveals that they have actually been approached by as many as ten companies who all want to become involved with Copella in some way or other; some they would feel quite happy to work with, while there are some they wouldn't touch with a barge pole.

I feel this is something of a diversion from my central point, and am not actually keen to press them on names and the kinds of deal being proposed. However, I do suspect that many of these companies have come up with deals which include the continuing involvement of the family because they probably feel that this is the only sort of deal that would be acceptable to them, given their previous attitude to takeovers. It also gives those members of the family who are wary of change an excuse for not really looking analytically at what lies ahead.

For Tamara and Stephen in particular, the choices are difficult. The idea of leaving a job which everyone says you are good at, for some nebulous future developing a business you don't know much about and in which you may not even be really interested, would make anyone feel uncertain and anxious.

Family firms are so tied up in themselves they always imagine if they just do a little more of the same, it will all come right in the end. It rarely does. Nine times out of ten you need to do something different. Nine times out of ten you have to stand back and look at the problem objectively.

And here? What do I feel I have achieved? I have brought the family so far, but I don't feel I have persuaded them to take the quantum leap necessary if they are to secure an interesting and profitable future for themselves as a family business. I have made them see what has happened to their fruit juice business, and how the future is unlikely to get any easier if they persist in going it alone.

The Peake family can feel justifiably proud of their achievement. Developing and establishing a major grocery brand in today's competitive climate is no mean achievement. The Copella brand is excellent and I am convinced it can prosper and grow, but I part company with the family about the best way of achieving this. I still think the family would be happier if they severed their links with the fruit juice business and let someone else develop the Copella brand.

The idea of developing the brand in partnership with another company is clearly an option attractive to the family. I just wonder how easy it would be for them to work with outsiders. I would really like to see the family concentrate their undoubted energies and talents on the leisure business. This is where the potential lies, but it's an operation which needs some very determined management and I don't think it will get the attention it deserves while the family continues its love affair with Copella.

It is obviously a very emotional time for the Peake family. They are standing at a crossroads. They are having to decide what to do with a product, Copella, and an enterprise, the fruit juice business, to which the whole culture and history of their family is inextricably linked. I want them to see that while fruit juices were a great growth business to be in during the 1970s and 1980s, they are now more or less flogging a dead horse and would be much better to hitch their wagon to their leisure business, the one part of their enterprise really capable of considerable growth well into the next century.

In August 1989, a month after my final visit to Boxford, I learnt that the Peakes had sold a majority stake in their fruit juice operation to Taunton Cider Company, the Dry Blackthorn and Autumn Gold cider company owned by a consortium of brewers – Bass, Courage, Scottish and Newcastle and Greene King. The company remains a separate entity within Taunton Cider. Susanna has been given the job of managing director, and Tamara and Stephen are staying on to do the sales and marketing. Taunton's initial plans are to retain Copella's apple processing operation at Boxford, and to repackage the Copella brand ready for a relaunch at the beginning of 1990.

This is clearly not the solution I would have opted for, but having failed to convince the family to be bold and radical and sever their links with their fruit juice operation, I am none the less pleased they have found a company they feel they can work with. Taunton Cider wants to develop the Copella brand and there are obvious opportunities for expanding it into pubs and off-licences. The Peakes have grown their business from an agricultural background and are strongly attached to the world of farming. This is something they feel they have in common with Taunton Cider which, although run by a group of big brewers, still has its roots very much in the Somerset countryside.

3

Apricot Computers

It doesn't seem so very long ago that home-grown computer companies like Apricot, Acorn and Sinclair Research were being mentioned in the same breath as US companies like IBM and Apple. It looked as if Britain was poised on the brink of a high-tech explosion which would catapult this new generation of computer companies, and their frequently vocal entrepreneurs, on to the world stage. So where are they now? Sir Clive Sinclair sold his range of home computers to Amstrad, Acorn were rescued by Olivetti and Apricot struggles on, lurching from one crisis to another.

These days you have to be addicted to the business section of your daily newspaper or the arcane pages of the specialist computer magazines to find the occasional titbit of information on Apricot and Roger Foster, its flamboyant founder, with his taste for flashy Albert Hall product launches complete with show biz stars, dancing girls and lots of dry ice. Otherwise you could be forgiven for thinking that Apricot had gone the way of Britain's other white heat hopes.

To give Apricot its due, it is nothing short of a miracle that it has survived. Apricot is not the only British company still making computers, but with the exception of ICL and Amstrad, which has only recently opened a factory in this country, it is the only one making computers in any volume. But it's a struggle. Nowadays most of Apricot's profits come not from making computers but from selling the programs that make them run, and from maintaining and repairing them.

Apricot went public in 1979, when it was still known as ACT, at the beginning of the personal computer boom. For the first few years, Apricot hardly put a foot wrong. In the early 1980s it backed a winner with the Sirius, a personal computer it bought in from the United States, and to begin with it did well with the first generation of Apricot machines which it manufactured at its own factory at Glenrothes in Scotland.

Much favoured by the share tipsters, Apricot's profits seemed to double every year and with it the company's shares. Then in 1986, the company was forced to admit it had made an enormous strategic blunder. Apricot's computers used programs which couldn't be used on IBM machines. Apricot was losing sales because it couldn't sell the range of programs offered by IBM and the other companies which had taken the IBM-compatible route.

Apricot took the bold decision to junk the old machines and redesign the range so it could run IBM programs. Profits went into freefall: that year there was a £26 million turnround, from profits of over £10 million to a loss of more than £15 million, a deficit which wiped out every penny of profits the company had ever earned.

The City is ruthless with its fallen angels. Apricot's shares followed profits into the Stygian depths. However, Apricot managed to pull back from the brink of oblivion. Profits recovered and Roger Foster was slowly regaining the trust of the City when, in January 1989, Apricot with its March year end approaching, issued a warning that profits would be lower than expected.

Trust is a fragile commodity in the City and there is no such thing as loyalty: once again the red ink was out, as dealers scrambled to rid themselves of Apricot's shares.

When it had time to reflect, the City decided once again that Apricot had lost its way. They judged there had been too many changes in direction; the range of computers, while technically advanced, was not designed with any particular marketing strategy in mind. Here was a company which promised a lot, but which continually failed to deliver the profits.

Roger Foster obviously feels under pressure. A City merchant bank has been buying shares in Apricot but refuses to tell him why. Roger Foster knows that, with Apricot's shares standing at such a low level on the stock market, Apricot is an easy takeover target, and the company he has led for nearly a quarter of a century could lose its independence.

A month before my first visit Apricot responded to City criticisms of its management with a big reshuffle of top personnel. Lindsey Bury, Roger Foster's long-time associate, is removed as non-executive chairman although he stays on the board as a director. Roger Foster moves up to executive chairman, and two new managing directors are appointed. Mike Hart is brought in from Nixdorf where he has been managing director of the UK operation for the previous four years, and Simon Hunt, who joined in 1985 as finance director from accountants Peat Marwick McLintock, is promoted.

Roger Foster is convinced that going all out for growth is Apricot's only hope of survival, and to do this the company must expand overseas. He sees the opportunities provided by 1992 and the opening up of European markets as his best hope of achieving this aim. Apricot wants my advice on how to achieve this, but I soon discover that before expansion can even be contemplated, the company's directors need to take a good hard look at their existing business and where it is heading.

Apricot's financial results (31 March year end)

	1980	1981	1982	1983	1984
Sales (£m)	5.6	7.2	8.4	22.8	50.8
Pre-tax profits (£m)	0.7	0.8	1.0	2.2	4.6
	1985	**1986**	**1987**	**1988**	**1989**
Sales (£m)	92.4	90.6	71.2	85.1	106.4
Pre-tax profits (loss) (£m)	10.6	−15.4	4.0	8.2	6.0

Apricot's headquarters is at Edgbaston in Birmingham, and as my taxi fights its way through traffic jams almost as dense as London's, I am in no doubt that the city is booming. My first appointment that wet May morning is with Mr Apricot himself, Roger Foster. I really need to know how he sees the business, where it is at the moment and where he wants to take it.

Roger Foster describes Apricot as a software and services company with a core business manufacturing computers. He has set Apricot the aim of having sales of £500 million in the 1994–95 financial year.

I want to know why Apricot remains so committed to making computers where the risk of getting things wrong and producing a machine that no one wants is so much greater than the reward for getting it right. In my view the potential risk does not match up to the potential reward, although I can see I may be thought a heretic for saying so.

Roger Foster is deeply committed to manufacturing, but I need to find out if this commitment is emotional or analytical. In any business, and especially a business closely identified with one individual as is the case with Apricot, it is difficult to deny your history. Having lived through the crisis of 1985–86 when £81 million of Apricot's £90 million sales came from personal computers and the company had no choice but to carry on manufacturing, it would obviously be hard for Roger Foster to give up on an activity which has absorbed so much of his time and emotional energy.

On the face of it this commitment to manufacturing is illogical. Apricot now has software and servicing activities which are much more profitable than making computers. In the year to the end of March 1989 computer manufacturing accounted for only two-thirds of sales and less than a fifth of profits, and contributed less than £2 of profit for every £100 of sales. And in the six months which followed, computer manufacturing actually lost money.

The question I have to answer is how dependent each activity is on all the others and what happens if you pull the rug on one activity: do the others come tumbling down like a house of cards?

Roger Foster describes the computers as the Trojan horse which creates the opportunity to sell a raft of higher-margin computer peripherals – monitors, printers and the like – and software. He says the services and maintenance operation, Apricot's single most profitable activity, owed its existence to the computers: the business developed from their customers' need to have their Apricot computers serviced and maintained.

I remain to be convinced, especially as, on Apricot's own admission, most of their big-money software packages, like Quasar and Citydesk, can operate on other makes of computer, and the computer graphics company, Sigmex, could operate independently of Apricot. Even the computer services operation is reducing its dependence on Apricot, with the move into servicing other makes of computer which followed the acquisition of DDT just six weeks prior to my first visit.

Taking this to its logical conclusion and accepting the idea that manufacturing may no longer be central to the main thrust of Apricot's changing business is something Roger Foster finds hard to take on board.

Maybe there is also an element of machismo in his desire to cling on to manufacturing. Roger Foster feels that British companies give up too easily, and that with the wealth of high-tech talent this country still seems able to produce he wants to be able to employ some of it in a home-grown company.

I suspect that the efforts of top management are entirely skewed towards manufacturing and that this is still the main focus of management energy within Apricot. My impression is confirmed when Roger Foster admits it probably takes up some two-thirds of his management time. He is not nearly so involved with the day-to-day management of the software and services operation where, he says, he manages the managers.

Roger Foster is very much the kind of manager who likes to roll up his sleeves and get stuck in. It's the team approach that works very well with small companies, where everyone needs to feel they are all part of the same dream. It's a style of management many managers find hard to shake off when their enterprises grow and become successful.

And yet management techniques have to change as companies change, and what is appropriate when a company is turning over £5 million is no longer appropriate when that turnover has grown to £100 million. I very much get the feeling that Roger Foster is still managing Apricot in the way he did ten years ago. On the computer manufacturing side he appears to involve himself in quite trivial decisions.

The trouble with bosses who get bogged down in detail is that they end up failing to do what they should be doing – directing the business. Companies the size of Apricot can't afford to just tick over with a management which is grappling only with the day-to-day issues. They must have a strategy, and it must be communicated to all levels of staff who, as well as knowing exactly what they are expected to contribute, should also have a very clear idea of the logic behind the company's thinking. It is then the board's job to see that the strategy is implemented.

Roger Foster obviously realises that Apricot's management style is no longer appropriate to its changing circumstances. He describes the recent management changes as the most significant for fifteen years. Mike Hart, one of two new managing diectors, brought in from Nixdorf, is the first manager Apricot has ever headhunted.

Roger Foster admits he always thought of strategic planning as something you did in spare moments at the weekend. His move from managing director to executive chairman is designed to give him more time to think and plan Apricot's future. I don't know whether he is going to find it easy to keep his distance from the detail and, metaphorically at least, keep his sleeves rolled down.

Like everyone else, Apricot has its eye on 1992, and Roger Foster is currently looking at ways to extend the company's presence in Europe. I am far from convinced that Apricot should start venturing abroad until it has a strategy in place for the home market which is seen to be working. His current idea is that the company should be attacking certain niche markets such as computer graphics through Sigmex, and financial software.

Niche markets are all very well, but unless you can be fairly sure of a dominant share of any particular niche, chasing them can involve a lot of work for little reward. And you are always exposed should your chosen niche suffer a sudden slump.

What I want to know is which bit is driving the business forward. Roger Foster says the computers are the Trojan horse which drag through the other sales. In fact I think the computers are more like Trojan mice, and at this stage I am still not sure that Apricot is looking at the problem from the right angle.

Even though computer manufacturing doesn't make much, or any, money for Apricot, Roger Foster sees it as the driving force which powers the company. I want to know if this view is shared by the managers in charge of the two activities which are actually earning the lion's share of Apricot's profits: computer services and financial systems.

Computer services are based 10 miles outside Birmingham at Oldbury. Chris Winn, who runs Apricot's computer services operation, shares Roger Foster's view that it could not exist without Apricot computers. But the new acquisition, DDT, has only been under his wing for six weeks, and although Chris Winn has already done all the sums, I don't think he has quite realised that the overall emphasis of Apricot's servicing business is changing. Chris still describes his job as adding value to Apricot's computers.

Before the acquisition of DDT, the computer services company employed 300 people and yearly sales were around £15 million. Some 60 per cent of the work is on Apricot computers, the rest involves all the computer peripherals that Apricot sells along with its computers: printers, monitors and disc drives, for example. Margins are higher on the work carried out on Apricots because parts and services are bought in from the rest of the group.

Just like everyone else within Apricot, Chris Winn is convinced that the servicing operation is entirely dependent on Apricot remaining a computer manufacturer.

At the time of my visit DDT and Apricot's computer services are still being run as two separate companies. Apricot has decided to integrate them although for marketing purposes hasn't yet decided if it is going to keep two separate identities or go for a new name.

Apricot had identified third-party maintenance and servicing as a potential area for acquisitions several years ago. It took a strategic stake in DDT in 1987, but it was only when another computer company, Wordplex, bid for the company that Apricot was forced to show its true intentions.

DDT has 300 employees and sales of around £7 million a year, but the margins are a lot lower than Apricot's. DDT is currently earning profits of around 5 per cent on sales; Apricot earns at least 20 per cent.

I am very impressed by Chris Winn's ability to focus on the bottom line, the actual profitability of the operation.

DDT has apparently been run by engineers, but Chris says he intends running it in a much more disciplined manner, and thinks it will be possible to push up the margin on third-party servicing to between 10 and 15 per cent. He reckons the computer servicing and maintenance market in the UK is worth around £63 million a year and that Apricot and DDT have something in the order of a 21 per cent share of that market.

Chris Winn has actually worked out what proportion of Roger Foster's £500 million he should be bringing in by 1994–95. He is aiming for 35–40 per cent, or around £160 million, and is working hard to maintain the margin earned on the Apricot contracts and increase it on those with third parties. He thinks if he really drives the company hard it could actually reach sales of £200 million with the help of some diversification and acquisitions.

I now need to find out if Mike Winn (no relation), the man in charge of Apricot's other big satellite operation, Apricot Financial Systems, shares Chris Winn's view that his business depends for its survival on the continuing existence of Apricot computers.

Apricot Financial Systems is based just down the road from Apricot's Edgbaston headquarters. Mike Winn confirms my impression that they operate almost autonomously and that the nature of the business is very different from the rest of Apricot. Apricot Financial Systems sells high-value software; the hardware is largely academic.

It wants to give the client a choice of hardware, so the software works on all the big-name computers. It is in the business of providing its clients with solutions, so it is a matter of asking clients what they want, and then providing it. One of its systems, Citydesk, was designed by Apricot with Apricot computers in mind, although even this product is capable of running on other computers.

Apricot Financial Systems began life as an in-house software operation which started offering its services outside the company. Now the business focuses on the growing financial services industry. Its top-selling Quasar software package is a back office fund management system used by all the major banks and investment groups.

The business, which had been growing fast, took a knock following the stock market crash of October 1987 when City firms put their investment plans on ice. Profits which reached a record £2.6 million in 1987–88 more than halved to £1.2 million the following year, before staging a recovery in the first half of 1989–90.

I ask Mike Winn what proportion of Roger's £500 million he intends to provide. He tells me he finds it difficult to think in terms of sales. As this is a low-sales, high-margin business, be prefers to gauge future performance in terms of profits, which is actually the way I think Roger Foster should be doing it. He expects Apricot Financial Systems to be making profits of £5 million in three years' time, from organic growth alone.

He expects the next five years to see a great deal of concentration among software companies, the main losers being medium-sized companies squeezed between the low costs of the 'mama and papa' businesses and the sophistication of the large companies. He wants to be a product-based company and has absolutely no intention of going down the route of some software and systems houses which are no more than sophisticated employment agencies, sending freelances into companies as and when they are needed. Mike Winn's dream is to become a financial supermarket used by firms of investment banks and stockbrokers because they know they will find there products to suit all their computing needs. He would like to expand faster, but this would entail making acquisitions, and Apricot's own position places constraints on Mike Winn's ability to do this. Apricot's lowly rated shares reduce its ability to finance takeovers with shares, and the company's history makes it unwilling to take on a high level of debt.

Mike Winn is exploring all sorts of other ventures. The financial services market is now expanding much faster in Europe than at home. Mike Winn obviously wants to exploit this opportunity, and I like his ideas for entering this market with a series of partners so that products can be shared.

I sense that Mike Winn clearly feels frustrated and slightly ill at ease working within the Apricot framework, a view which subsequently proves to be correct. He would like the company to grow fast to the stage where it could actually be making profits of £10 million in three years' time. He doesn't consider that the parent company contributes much to his operation, and over the previous couple of months has even suggested to the board ways in which the financial services company could be cut loose from Apricot.

I think the idea certainly has some merit. If Apricot reduced its stake in its financial systems company, it could offer potential European partners a stake in the business.

Mike Hart has only been at Apricot for two weeks, but I am more than a little interested in the views of someone who isn't steeped in the Apricot culture. I was immediately impressed. He described his job at Nixdorf as selling business solutions; he didn't elaborate with complicated explanations of the innards of a computer or the intricacies of the software.

Apricot is the largest supplier of personal computers to the government, with an alleged 35 per cent of that market, and they have recently won two large contracts: from the National Audit Office, and from the Department of Social Services.

Mike Hart wants Apricot to put a lot more effort into winning big corporate contracts, and to do this he feels the company is going to have to change the way it sells. He wants Apricot to start looking at what it is selling from the buyer's point of view. Almost every industry has problems that computers can solve: it's Apricot's job to isolate the industries where there is an opportunity and then design computer systems and software which that industry will find hard to resist. He wants those systems running on Apricot computers and hopes that the software can be Apricot's too. But on these big contracts, he says, the important point is to be accepted as the prime contractor, the company which puts forward and co-ordinates the installation of a complete computer system and then gets it up and running.

I also like Mike Hart's optimism. There is a slight feeling of 'Oh, wouldn't it be nice if we could . . .' about the rest of the company, but when Mike Hart says he believes Apricot can become one of Europe's leading computer companies, you believe him.

I end my first day at Apricot back in Roger Foster's office, where I run through my impressions with him. We talk about the culture of the company. I like the open, friendly and relatively unstuffy atmosphere. The place has style; the people who work here believe in the company and the product; and they see themselves as carrying a little Union Jack for their country.

But the other side is that I get no sense of urgency, and

there is a general lack of focus. I am not sure that Roger Foster's sales target of £500 million for the 1994–95 financial year is ambitious enough, and I mistrust targets measured in sales. I want Apricot to set its target in terms of how much profit it can earn. I think the company must pass through the narrows and go for very fast expansion because I don't think time is on its side. I am worried that people don't seem to be stressed up enough, and although no one is actually sitting around with their feet up reading the newspaper, no one really gives the impression of working their butt off either.

There is no doubt that Roger Foster does see the problem, but he is like the servant with two masters. On the one hand he wants to encourage Apricot down the systems, networking and services route, but on the other he has a factory which needs to churn out personal computers, albeit rather classy ones.

I am still uncertain whether Apricot should remain in manufacturing. Although Roger Foster has grasped the nature of the problems facing Apricot, I don't think he is going to find it easy to change. My main hopes rest with Mike Hart, although I think he will meet a certain amount of resistance to change when he tries to bring in the policies he thinks he has been recruited to implement.

Apricot is Roger Foster's baby. And of course he loves his baby. But is he going to allow his baby to walk out of the house, get educated and earn its own living or is he going to keep it bouncing on his knee?

I still want to know why Apricot can't make money making computers. They make these lovely machines which run the same software as the IBM, they add extra features which make them more sophisticated than the IBM, and then they go out into the marketplace and sell them for less. It doesn't make sense, and I want to know why.

In an attempt to find the answers I arrange to visit the factory and fix up a couple of meetings with a computer expert and some Apricot dealers.

Cutting the cost of production might be one way of increasing Apricot's profits from manufacturing. Ron Birse, the factory general manager, and main board director, Peter Oldershaw, take me around Apricot's factory in Glenrothes, in what has become known as Scotland's Silicon Glen.

The factory is organised along lines that I very much support, and I like the open and democratic feel of the place. Everyone gets the same employment package: there are no extra perks for the managers; everyone eats in the same canteen and there is no clocking on. Demarcation disputes are avoided by paying the assembly, inspection, stores and clerical staff the same wages; this also gives Apricot the flexibility to switch staff around.

The factory is currently working at way below its full capacity. At the height of the personal computer boom it turned out 6000 Apricots a month. Now, with just one shift, that figure is between 3000 and 4000, and there is capacity for producing twice or even three times as many machines.

Once bitten, twice shy, and after the experience of 1985–86 when the company was left with a whole load of stock it couldn't sell, the factory now basically only makes what it can sell, and prides itself on getting the machines to the dealers quicker than anyone else. This is not the most efficient method of manufacturing, but with labour accounting for only 5 per cent of manufacturing costs, Apricot feels that not having to worry about stock levels is worth the loss of efficiency. The company also thinks that being able to respond quickly to customers' demands gives it an advantage over companies which bring in finished machines from the Far East, where the delivery pipeline is six to eight weeks, and where there is a greater risk of being left with unsold stock.

The cost of components accounts for up to 90 per cent of the cost of making an Apricot computer. Component ordering is done from Glenrothes, and for such a small company, Apricot appears to have a good relationship with its suppliers. Cynics would say this is because major component suppliers know that Apricot likes to be among the first to introduce new products, so they use the company to test their components in a quiet corner of the market where they are unlikely to be noticed if something goes wrong.

Apricot may have good relations with its suppliers, but with components accounting for up to 90 per cent of its costs, in the end it is price which counts. Small companies like Apricot lack clout and don't normally get a good deal from their suppliers, which in turn restricts their ability to compete on price in the market place.

I find my visit to the factory has still failed to clarify the problems for me. Half Apricot's sales come from selling computers, and yet the profits it earns from this activity are negligible. Roger Foster's Trojan horse theory is all well and good, but when I talk to Mike Winn at Apricot's Financial Systems I find someone who is distancing himself from reliance on Apricot, and since the acquisition of DDT, the computer maintenance and servicing operation has also become less dependent on the sales of Apricot computers.

Apricot is caught in all sorts of cleft sticks. It has a good reputation with its suppliers because it is keen to take on all the latest untested technology. This gives Apricot superior products but not the ability to charge for them. If it were producing a more basic product, the margin wouldn't necessarily be any better because as a small predominantly UK producer Apricot wouldn't carry much clout with its suppliers. And with only 5 per cent of production costs attributable to labour, it doesn't seem to me that Apricot has much scope for increasing profits by cutting costs.

It is now time to test my impressions against the opinions of the outside world. I have arranged to meet Guy Kewney, a specialist computer writer, at ITEC, a computer training centre in London's Covent Garden. Sadly, he is not very optimistic. He admires Apricot's technology, but agrees with Apricot that the company is in no position to charge for it. Apparently this is the way the market has developed over the last couple of years: anyone who wants to compete with IBM has to charge less and offer more. All I can say is, no wonder the personal computer market is in such a mess.

Guy Kewney says Apricot hasn't spent – or hasn't wanted to spend – the money on marketing its computers. He worries about the quality of computer dealers in general, and Apricot's in particular. Overall, the number of dealers is shrinking, and many are reducing the number of makes they stock: with major companies like Atari, Philips, Commodore and Olympia all poised to make an assault on the market, what chance does a company like Apricot have?

It doesn't seem that it has a particularly good relationship with the dealers it does have. While Apricot may be good at delivering computers the following day, the company has a terrible reputation for keeping its dealers in the dark. Apricot recently took the decision to do some of the selling itself rather than channel all its sales through the dealer network. I am not sure that some of the larger dealers are going to be very pleased by this decision.

Most of Apricot's dealers sell to the small business market. Guy Kewney wants to know how Apricot is going to attack the corporate market where it will need to be if it is going to make a success of being the first company to produce a clone of the new IBM personal computer.

I have arranged to meet a small group of dealers who have stuck with Apricot through thick and thin and who have built their business around selling Apricot's products. There is a strong feeling that being British helps Apricot. Given the choice between two companies offering roughly similar products, many clients, such as local authorities, will buy British. People also like the security of knowing that if anything goes wrong they can pick up the phone and talk to the designer which, according to the dealers, Apricot is always prepared to let them do.

They also claim that Apricot's advanced technology helps them sell the computers. Even if the client doesn't necessarily need it and has no intention of using it, nobody likes to feel they have bought outdated technology.

It is my feeling that Apricot is trying to provide something for everyone and as a result its marketing, and how it is perceived in the marketplace, appears to lack focus. The dealers I met were generally critical of Apricot's below-the-line promotional expenditure. They would like Apricot to run promotional seminars designed to attract a particular industry.

From the dealers' point of view, the problems of dealing with Apricot are often more niggling than strategic. For example, it is not unheard of for Apricot to change its published prices three times in the course of a month. And there is difficulty in getting day-to-day decisions out of the company, because even trivial matters have to be taken to Roger Foster.

The dealers were genuinely impressed by Apricot's much-vaunted delivery system. They agree it does work, and an order put in at 4 o'clock in the afternoon is generally there by 10 o'clock the next morning.

The dealers expressed a high level of anxiety about the company's intentions towards them as they develop their own direct sales force. They have been told that Roger Foster is aiming for sales of £500 million by 1994–95, but no one has told them how much of that business the dealers are expected to produce.

Apricot doesn't appear to be communicating effectively with its dealers, who feel they are being left out of detailed dicussions on the company's strategy. The feeling is that the company is either leaving them in the dark, or worse, that it doesn't actually have a definite marketing plan. Whichever it is, the dealers are worried.

My concern is that while the company has a core of dedicated dealers who believe in the gospel according to Apricot, it needs more high-calibre dealers, and these may be difficult to recruit. Mergers and takeovers among the larger dealers is leading to increased concentration among the top-notch dealers, and they are going to be less prepared to do business with small fry like Apricot.

Since it is based in Birmingham, Apricot has developed a northern bias. Two-thirds of its dealers are based north of the Wash, and this two-thirds/one-third split is also reflected in sales. Attracting more dealers in the south is an obvious priority. Apricot Financial Systems has a London office in Pall Mall, but this isn't used by the rest of Apricot. The sales team have been promised, and need, a London base but the strong streak of financial cautiousness which runs through Apricot's top management has somehow prevented this from happening.

It is now a month since I made my first visit to Apricot, and it is time to make my return visit to the company. We agree to meet at New Hall, a hotel converted from a moated manor house, on the outskirts of Sutton Coldfield, and Roger Foster and I take a walk round the splendid garden.

Roger Foster has failed to convince me that Apricot is not yet in a position to pull out of computer manufacturing, an activity which takes up the majority of top management's time, earns practically no profit, and in the first half of 1989–90 was actually losing them money. If Apricot is intent on staying in manufacturing it must expand its way out of its immediate problems, but in a way which allows for damage limitation if the strategy goes wrong.

I see no immediate solution to the company's problems, and as in all the other companies I visited for this television series, I find myself wanting to shake the management and tell them to be more ambitious. But in Apricot's case they need to perceive their own position more clearly, and define precisely where they are going.

My first concern is organisational and this is a job only Roger Foster can tackle. Apricot's board has been used as a reward for good behaviour. It gets bogged down in taking too many detailed organisational decisions, and doesn't address itself to issues of strategy.

I suggest a smaller board of three non-executive directors, plus Roger Foster as chairman. Below this level there could be an operating board, if this was found necessary.

It is always a mistake to have two managing directors. Roger Foster thinks it may be useful while Apricot is making this transition to its new management structure. I try to convince him that this stage should be as short as possible, and he must aim to have only one managing director before six months is up. The danger inherent in having two managing directors is that effectively it allows Roger Foster to slip into the void between the two, where he can stay on as *de facto* managing director.

Apricot doesn't have the board it deserves, and I am not sure that Roger Foster fully understands the issues with which a chairman and a board of directors should be concerning themselves.

In my view the first job of a chairman is managing the board. It is the work of the board to plan the company's strategy and then see it is carried out. Like it or not, the chairman also has a public relations role: not just in the accepted sense, where the company makes contact with the world outside, but also internally to make sure everyone working for the company has received the message, shares it and feels responsibility for it.

I think Roger Foster knows, at least intellectually, that he must take a step away from the day-to-day management of Apricot, and that he must now be the guy who metaphorically spends his days with the wet towel over his head gazing soulfully into the future.

However, there is a stubborn part of him which remains almost glued to the bit of Apricot which manufactures computers. This is without doubt the single most problematic part of Apricot and, perhaps not unnaturally, he feels if he hands over the management to someone else they are likely to make an even bigger mess of it.

I find the working atmosphere at Apricot on the whole relaxed, unstressed and rather unmotivated, and I think Roger Foster is genuinely surprised that an outsider sees

Apricot in this way. Part of the problem of having a company where most decisions are made by the man at the top is that it robs the managers below him of their ability to manage, and they become either demoralised or complacent.

The only area where there is any evidence of drive and ambition is in product development, where everyone clearly does feel under pressure to produce the next computer ahead of the competition.

It is essential that Roger Foster starts defining Apricot's financial goals in terms of profits, not sales. He has committed himself to a sales target of £500 million by 1994–95, but has never indicated what level of profit that implies. Is he aiming for profits of £100 million or £10 million? I have no idea.

Roger Foster and I are now joined by Simon Hunt and Mike Hart. I start with my analysis of Apricot. As has happened so often during the making of this television series, this has ended up covering different ground than the company originally expected.

Apricot had asked me for advice on how to tackle the European market and the challenge of 1992. After looking at Apricot, I think the move into Europe is largely irrelevant until the company has a better grip and a clearer focus on its all-important home market. I want to impress on them that I am worried about their future. I think they must attack their problems with a greater sense of urgency. I share Roger Foster's view that the company must go for growth, but that growth must be defined in terms not of sales, but of profits.

I have turned Roger Foster's sales target of £500 million by 1994–95 into a profit target of £50 million, and I want them to achieve this figure in three years, not five. I think it will be tough but I am sure they can do it. I reiterate my point about the relaxed, unstressed feeling which prevails throughout Apricot. The company has some excellent people but they have not been made to feel in any way responsible for the future success of the enterprise and somehow the whole culture of the place must change to one more motivated by profit.

Apricot has two businesses, the financial software operation and the services and maintenance operation, which are both capable of strong growth. The services and maintenance business is already strongly profit-motivated and has a good idea of where it is going, although it could probably dare to be a bit more ambitious. The financial software company has good products which, in spite of a temporary hiccup, are selling into internationally growing markets. The business needs a sharper focus, but there should be no problem achieving this.

In the end all the real question marks hang over the computer manufacturing operation. Marketing is in a mess, the company is trying to make the difficult transition from selling only through dealers to a position where they also have a direct sales force.

Apricot knows that to survive it must target sales on the higher-margin solution-solving end of the market rather than the low-margin volume end. But at the moment Apricot has only a handful of dealers competent to service this market, and it needs a far larger number. Nor is it going to be easy to recruit dealers of the quality it needs, when companies the size of Compaq, Olivetti and Atari are now better known than the home-grown competitor.

Taking each bit of Apricot in detail, I start with the financial systems operation. I am impressed with this operation. It is a good indication of what Apricot can do if it really attacks a niche market. It also enjoys the advantage of operating independently of the rest of Apricot, and is in no way dependent on the sale of Apricot computers. The only problem is that the company appears to have captured some 60 per cent of the UK market which may restrict its ability to grow.

And although I don't advise that Apricot should contemplate satisfying what I describe as its Euro-itch, I make an exception for the financial systems company. In fact I think it essential that they expand their operations into Europe. This is likely to involve partnerships with other companies to form a pan-European financial software company, which would probably be best achieved by cutting the company free, with Apricot retaining a stake of, say, 40 per cent.

I move on to the services and maintenance business. Chris Winn who manages the business is about the only manager in Apricot who has his eye firmly fixed on the bottom line profit figures. He is very ambitious, so much so that he feels he can grow his part of the business to the stage where it is earning profits of £40 million by 1994–95. I am still not sure how much this business is and will continue to be dependent on the fact that Apricot actually makes computers.

We are now at the point where we must look at the kernel of Apricot's problem and how the company has got itself caught on the horns of all sorts of dilemmas.

Apricot has a reputation for being at the cutting edge of all new computer developments. It likes to be among the first to bring out any new generation of computer product, and generally succeeds, although sometimes at the expense of reliability. For a company Apricot's size, this involves costly investment in research and development. The company is constantly introducing new models, it rarely achieves great volume on any of them and it is unclear whether to chase volume or margin.

It seems to be the received wisdom in the computer world that Apricot will get nowhere unless it gives more and charges less for it. I really need to challenge to destruction the notion that manufacturing is the steel cord running through Apricot which knits the whole lot together.

Is it really necessary for Apricot to manufacture and design its own machines? I want to know if it might not make more sense to import a basic IBM clone, probably from the Far East, and then customise it at the Glenrothes factory for specially developed niche markets. This would have the effect of freeing management resources which are currently disproportionately tied up in manufacturing. Managers would then be free to develop the corporate market, where companies are more interested in finding solutions to their business problems than they are in the name on the computer.

I don't feel I have convinced them to take a fundamental look at Apricot's position as a manufacturer, and maybe psychologically this is not the right time to do it. Roger Foster has only just announced the launch of the Titan, the first computer to be powered by Intel's new 486 processor, which he has described as Apricot's most important new product ever.

They are determined to go for volume, and if this is the case they must spend a lot more time and effort on their marketing: recruiting more dealers, making sure they are properly trained, and developing a high-quality direct sales force. But as they do this, I want them to be making a big effort to continue the process they have already begun of shifting the emphasis away from hardware towards software, and providing solutions to business problems.

If they are developing a two- to three-year strategy to grow the hardware part of their business, I advise them to devise an exit plan should it all go wrong and they find reaching that critical mass is just an impossible dream, or their product range flops. If, as they push for hardware growth, they also continue to shift the emphasis of the overall business towards software and services, then at least they will have a viable business to fall back on if they do, as I suspect they will have to, bow out of manufacturing.

I am worried about Apricot's future, and I don't want to see the company martyring itself on the cross of computer manufacturing when it has two sound businesses with a lot going for them which deserve a bigger share of top management attention. To my mind Roger Foster is treading a perilous path and as I left him, Mike Hart and Simon Hunt to their lunch, I didn't feel my message had got through.

But as the events of the next six months unfolded it became clear that my time at Apricot had not been wasted. Far from it. Of all the companies I visited for this television series, Apricot is the one that appears to have been the most influenced by my thinking, even if at the time my views were greeted with scepticism.

Just as I hoped, Apricot is continuing to rapidly expand its software and its servicing and maintenance activities. In the middle of October 1989 Apricot took over the loss-making ITL. A computer company in many ways similar to Apricot, ITL had sales of around £31.6 million in 1989. The loss of £1.2 million was mainly due to the company's decision to change the design of its computer to an industry standard.

But it wasn't ITL's computer manufacturing that attracted Apricot. The plum was the company's software and services operation, which takes Apricot into new markets such as health administration and computer maintenance.

Apricot has also taken steps to beef up the marketing of the computers. Brian Androlia and Ed Sherman, the two sales directors who had been with Apricot since the early days, left. The move into direct selling was abandoned in favour of an in-house sales team, called enablers, who are to work with the dealers on the larger corporate contracts.

I was sad to see the company lose Mike Winn, who headed Apricot Financial Systems, and whose ability had impressed me. However, it did appear that he wanted to pull the financial systems company in directions which the rest of the board were unhappy about.

And in January 1990 Roger Foster announced a major reorganisation. Apricot's computer manufacturing business has been put into play, in what looks to me like an exit strategy. Roger Foster wants an overseas partner to take a stake in Apricot's computer manufacturing business. The stated aim is to help Apricot develop overseas markets. Should he succeed in his search for a partner, it will reduce Apricot's reliance on computer manufacturing and the financial risk which that involves.

But what I find most exciting is the new emphasis now being given to software and services. Mike Hart is to head a new Apricot subsidiary, ACT, which is to be responsible for all Apricot's software and services operations.

I always got the impression that Roger Foster saw software and services as peripheral to the main business of making computers. At last it seems to have dawned on Apricot that these activities must now be the engine which drives Apricot forward, and that computer manufacturing must take a back seat. Instead of shunting software and services up a management siding, they are now to get the depth and quality of management which was previously reserved for manufacturing.

I am convinced that the future for a company like Apricot lies in its ability to design computer systems which solve business problems. It is no longer simply a matter of shifting boxes, or designing software and hoping someone will buy it. Business customers expect more these days. They need computer people who understand the nature of their business, who can come up with computer solutions and who are round within the hour if anything goes wrong.

I am now hopeful for Apricot. It is making the all-important cultural change from seeing itself as a computer manufacturer, and a failing one at that, to a hopefully highly successful computer software and services company. My only sadness is that the City is taking these changes at Apricot with a large dash of salt. The shares which had been bobbing around the 65p mark for the previous six months moved up to around 70p after the announcement, but this may not be enough to scare off any potential predator.

The danger is very real, and Roger Foster admits to feeling threatened. Merchant bankers Singer & Friedlander have recently increased their stake in Apricot to just over 16 per cent. They say they are buying on their own account and intend taking the stake up to 20 per cent. Has the bank some grand design for restructuring Britain's computer industry? Whatever the reason, Roger Foster would like to know, but so far the bank has refused all invitations to explain its motives.

4

Morgan Motor Company

Few cars excite so much attention and command so much loyalty among drivers as the Morgan. There is a 1950s glamour about the car. The appeal is dripping in nostalgia. It conjures up images of wholesome Grace Kelly lookalikes with Hermès scarves, and clean-shaven young men in tweed sports jackets off for a spin in the country.

Marketing people use nostalgia quite cynically to sell everything from jam, to soap, to luggage. The product may be the same as a supermarket brand sold at half the price, but with the help of some pretty packaging we are quite prepared to be conned into believing that we are keeping alive some ancient craft.

Morgan is different. Here the appeal to the nostalgic is not just skin deep. The Morgan is not the product of the fertile mind of some marketing man – it is the real thing. With Morgan it is not just the car which is caught in a time warp, the factory itself has all the period charm of a sepia photograph from some bygone age when car workers were recruited from the village and there was much touching of forelocks when the boss walked through the shopfloor. The Morgan factory is very far removed in time from a modern car assembly line.

The Morgan is a hand-built car, which accounts for

much of its charm. The trouble is that if you want a new one, your name goes on a waiting list, and you can still be waiting ten years later. Morgan makes around 430 cars a year. Half are exported, which leaves just over 200 cars a year to satisfy what on the face of it appears to be an insatiable demand for the car in the country of its birth.

The Morgan management wanted my advice on how they could solve the seemingly impossible task of increasing production without risking Morgan's reputation for producing hand-built cars.

The history of the Morgan stretches back through three generations of the Morgan family. The company, which was founded in Malvern in 1910 by the legendary H. F. S. Morgan, is still owned by the Morgan family. H. F. S. Morgan's son Peter was still running the company when I first became involved. His son Charles had recently joined the company, after a successful career as an ITN cameraman.

The company's fortunes were founded on a cheap and cheerful three-wheeler car, known as the Morgan Runabout, which enjoyed tremendous success up to the middle of the 1920s. At one time the factory in Malvern, which is still in use today, managed to turn out a record 2300 cars a year, more than five times the number the factory now produces. The classic Morgan sports car on which the Morgan reputation now rests was first introduced in 1935 and apart from the introduction of a version with a V8 engine at the end of the 1960s, the car has remained essentially the same since the late 1930s.

The length of the waiting list is the one thing most people know about Morgan. But how long do you actually have to wait for a Morgan? If you want a straight answer don't ask Morgan. On the record Peter Morgan says the waiting list is four or five years. But rumour has it that Morgan is still completing orders received up to ten years ago.

Peter Morgan does worry about the waiting list. He knows that many potential customers are put off buying a Morgan because of the wait. For example the Italians love the car, but always want it straight away. Apparently British buyers are more phlegmatic. However, he says he would be equally worried if the delay was less than six months. He remembers his father telling him always to make sure that demand is always slightly ahead of supply.

The reasons for this extraordinary state of affairs are not hard to find. Morgan has survived as a small car manufacturer against all the odds. It has lived through the kind of peaks and troughs of demand which forced most of their contemporaries out of business or into the arms of the mass production giants. The waiting list is Morgan's insurance that, if all else fails, at least they have orders enough to carry them through the next ten years.

As a small boy Peter Morgan can recall periodic bad times, particularly in the mid-1920s when demand for the three-wheeler collapsed following the appearance of the Austin Seven. He remembers walking through the factory when most of the cars were ticketed for stock, and wondering why Mr Stock needed so many cars. These memories of bad times are obviously deeply felt, and appear to have affected the development of the company at the kind of psychological level which is rarely taken into account when the history of a company is told.

Morgan has even weathered downturns in demand during Peter Morgan's time with the company. Peter joined the company at the end of the Second World War, during the period of postwar austerity when food rationing was at its most savage. There was not a lot of money left over for luxuries, and demand for Morgans was negligible. The factory, which had been turned over to making munitions during the war, had only just started making cars again, and the company was saved from extinction when it found there was demand for the car abroad.

When the company's founder, H. F. S. Morgan, died in 1959 as much as 85 per cent of all Morgans were going to the United States. At home the car was considered old-fashioned and orders hit a new low. It was against this background that Peter Morgan took over as chairman, and his first move was to develop a new covered car with a fibreglass body for the home market. It flopped, a failure which still haunts him and has clearly influenced the company's chosen path of never tampering with the traditional Morgan look.

Crisis struck the company again at the end of the 1960s. The decade of the Beatles and the Rolling Stones saw classic cars such as the Morgan and the MG swing back into fashion in the UK. Mick Jagger and Brigitte Bardot, two archetypal sixties figures, are both reputed to have owned Morgans. But in the States it was also the decade of Ralph Nader and aggressive consumerism. This led to stiff new emission controls for cars which British-made sports cars were unable to meet at an economic cost. As a result, US sales of Morgan cars collapsed overnight. Fortunately demand for the car at home and in other export markets was sufficient to pick up the slack. The car and the V8 version which was introduced around this time have remained popular and in demand ever since.

Morgan owners are fanatically loyal. They nickname the car Mog, or Moggie, and call themselves the Morganatics. On Morgan's 75th birthday in 1984 they organised a rally.

More than 1200 cars turned up at Malvern from as far afield as America, Japan, Cyprus, Sweden, Spain and Poland. There are collectors who spend every spare moment tracking down some rarity or cataloguing refinements.

If your name is on the Morgan waiting list and your number comes up, it's your car from the beginning of the three-month manufacturing process. You choose the colour, the type of upholstery, the extras. You are even welcome in the factory to give your car a pat or two during the time it is being made.

There are dark stories of people speculating on the Morgan waiting list. With so much pent-up demand for the car, a place near the front of the Morgan queue is obviously worth a considerable sum of money, and it is not unknown for people to trade their place in the queue. Morgan discourages the practice by making only for the customer named on the list and insisting that the car is not delivered until it has been registered in that customer's name.

However, it is not uncommon to see Morgans advertised with 'delivery-only mileage', at a premium of between 15 and 20 per cent above the list price, so even if Morgan dislikes the fact that there is a speculative element on their waiting list, it is powerless to stamp it out.

Morgan makes money but the company may need to be more profitable to guarantee its survival. As the following figures show, sales in the ten years to May 1989 grew from £2 286 000 to £5 331 000, and pre-tax profits rose from £247 000 to £488 000. On the face of it this looks a more creditable performance, but further analysis reveals that, with the exception of 1989, profits have only exceeded those achieved in 1980 in three years.

Companies making luxury goods – and I would put

Morgan in this category – can normally expect to make a very healthy return on their sales: a figure of 15–20 per cent is what most companies in this category would aim for. Compare Morgan against this yardstick and it becomes clear that the company is not performing as well as it ought to. For every £100 worth of sales, Morgan was only making £5.60 worth of profit in 1988, and even in 1989 when profits nearly doubled (figures which hadn't yet been prepared during my visits to the company), the return was only £9.15. This is well short of the desired level and quite inadequate to sustain and develop the business.

However, having said that, at current levels of profitability Morgan has sufficient cash flow to finance its current methods of operation without borrowing from the bank.

Morgan is still entirely owned by the family. At the time of my first visits to the company, Peter Morgan is the chairman of a seven-strong board, of whom four including himself are members of the Morgan family. And it really is a family affair. Charles was made a director when he joined the family firm in 1986. His mother Jane, and Peter's second wife, Heather, also sit on the board, even though they play no active part in the day-to-day management of the company. Peter and Charles own over 75 per cent of the shares, the rest being held by other members of the family.

In the run-up to my first visit to the factory, Morgan has set itself various targets and wants my opinion on how to set about achieving them. The company knows it ought to increase production, and Morgans have set themselves the apparently modest aim of upping the number of cars produced each week from 9 to 10.

Charles Morgan has managed to persuade the rather

Financial results (31 May year end)

	1980	1981	1982	1983	1984
Sales (£000)	2286	2662	2762	3002	3184
Pre-tax profits (£000)	247	187	143	121	34
	1985	**1986**	**1987**	**1988**	**1989**
Sales (£000)	n.a.	n.a.	n.a.	4827	5331
Pre-tax profits (£000)	251	179	293	283	488

reluctant workforce to produce 10 cars a week on a three-week trial basis. Their reluctance is not hard to understand. They have been promised extra money if they succeed, but no one knows exactly how much more they will get in their pay packets.

This is not the first time the management has exhorted the shopfloor to produce more cars. However, previous attempts have always failed, because although most of the workshops succeed, the whole process is let down by hold-ups in one or two areas. One or two extra cars get built every month for a time and then production slips back into its old comfortable pattern.

Although there seems to be general management agreement that this modest increase in production is necessary, I get the feeling there may be some disagreements about the long-term direction of the company. I want to know if I can unravel some of these tensions.

My impression even before visiting the factory is that Morgan's problems are rather more fundamental than simply increasing production, and I approach the company in a fairly critical state of mind.

In a way Morgan has the problem of success. The car has a tremendous following, it generates great enthusiasm, and there is the enormous waiting list. The car sells all over the world, and half the output is exported. But I sense that the company really isn't going anywhere and, sadly, companies which don't go anywhere are usually heading for trouble. In my view increasing production by one car a week isn't going to have much impact on the waiting list. It's just tinkering with the problem.

And given the opportunities the company has, it doesn't appear to be making a high enough level of profits. The old-fashioned way in which the car is manufactured is undoubtedly a problem. Labour accounts for about a third of the cost of producing it. That's a very high figure and it is likely to increase as time goes on. It is a manufacturer's job to continually seek to reduce costs and produce a better product.

If Morgan doesn't tackle this problem sooner or later then eventually the car will become uncompetitive because labour costs will be growing faster than those of competitors with a lower labour content. On the face of it everything is rosy. In reality I think there are much deeper underlying problems. I suspect that the whole culture of the company is against change but, unless they do change, I think that slowly but inevitably the company will decline.

None the less I start my visit tremendously enthusiastic about the company, and I really want to see it succeed. As a boy I yearned for the day when I could own a Morgan three-wheeler. Morgan obviously has a great deal going for it. It has a much coveted product, exports half of everything it makes, has a loyal and dedicated workforce and a close relationship with Morgan owners. It is just the sort of business Britain needs more of.

I finally make my appearance at Morgan's Malvern factory one crisp sunny winter's day in March 1989.

I meet all the senior management, and the shop stewards, and manage to talk to a number of the shopfloor workers as I go round the factory. I see Peter Morgan and his son Charles separately, which gives me some idea of how they both see the problems and challenges of Morgan and how their views vary. The works manager, Mark Aston, who is also Peter Morgan's personal assistant, takes me on a tour of the factory during the course of which I meet Geoff Margetts, the company secretary who is also responsible for financial control, Derek Day the sales director, Bill Warwin, who is in charge of stocks, and Maurice Owen, the chief development engineer.

I also get to sample the Morgan magic, when they give me a Morgan Plus 8, the model with Austin Rover V8 engine, to test drive. It takes me a while to get the hang of the gearbox, and I am not sure I would ever get used to the bumpy ride, but there is an undeniable romance about this car, and it's not hard to see how people get hooked.

The factory gives the impression of being run by a bunch of enthusiastic amateurs. Mark Aston, the works manager, also deals with the service department and any warranty claims. He describes himself as a Morgan person. He got his job at Morgan not because he is a trained engineer, but simply because he loves everything about the car. As I walk round, it becomes clear that there is no logical flow of production through the factory, and very little production planning.

The shopfloor workers are paid a basic wage, and a production bonus which generally accounts for around half their weekly wage. However, the bonus doesn't work as incentive, as hiccups in the production flow often slow things up somewhere else in the process of making the completed car. The foremen are paid more but they aren't paid anything extra if their workers increase production so they have no incentive to exhort the men to work harder.

The machine shop, where bought-in castings are worked, is antique, badly undercapitalised and in need of some fresh investment – I haven't seen so many ancient machines since I was a boy.

The layout of the factory is historic, and apparently hasn't changed much since 1919 when the original factory was extended. There are plans to amalgamate the wiring and wing-fitting shops, but this is just tweaking at the problem, and falls a long way short of the complete overhaul that the whole factory really needs.

Mark Aston has been with Morgan thirteen years, but it seems like thirty. He does see the need for some change to the way the car is made, but basically likes the way things are at the moment: it is almost as if Morgan blood ran through his veins. I was disappointed to see someone as young and bright as Mark so lacking in flexibility.

Derek Day, the sales director, finds it hard to think of making beyond 450–500 cars a year. In fact, he is not what most people would call a sales director; he hasn't actually had to sell a car for twenty years. Derek is effectively Morgan's customer liaison man. When your number comes up on the Morgan waiting list, it's Derek who writes to find out which model you want, and what the car is to look like. It's Derek you deal with when you decide on the colour of your Morgan and the kind of upholstery and wheels to have fitted.

Morgan's sales department is production led. They don't

think in terms of how many they can sell, but how many they can produce. Derek Day is in effect a rationer of cars, not a sales director at all. The company is introducing a clean-burn engine which would meet United States regulations, but is doing this without any idea of how many cars they could sell over there.

Morgan has a good spread of export markets. Germany, Italy and Japan are currently the most important overseas markets with 50–60 cars a year going to two agents in Germany. But Derek Day doesn't know what would happen to demand for the car in all these markets if they put the price up.

The June 1989 UK price list shows prices before extras of between £12 645 for the basic 1600 two-seater model up to £19 528 for the Plus 8 petrol injection model. These prices look reasonable when compared with those of Panther, perhaps Morgan's nearest competitor, which charges £13 300 for its basic model, and Aston Martin which, although not directly comparable, have the same sort of cachet in the classic car market, and where the basic model will knock you back £120 000.

There is a healthy second-hand market for Morgans and the fact that you can sell a Morgan for more than you paid for it seems to indicate that price could be increased without affecting demand; in any case demand so far outstrips supply that testing the elasticity of the market need not be high-risk.

There is a lack of precision about the data the sales department collects, and getting any hard figures out of Derek Day is not an easy task. I end up suggesting figures to which he can agree, but I never feel confident that I have an accurate picture of what he thinks the demand is.

We agree that new orders are between 600 and 800 a

year, and that the waiting list is around 3600 cars. My conclusion is that even if Morgan increased production to 600 cars a year, up to 200 cars a year would still be added to their waiting list. But Derek Day doesn't actually see anything wrong in having a waiting list. He concedes it may now be too long; he would like to see it reduced to between two and three years, but anything less would scare him.

And seeing it from his point of view, why should things change? The cars sell themselves, he doesn't actually have to do anything to get the orders in. He has been dealing with some customers for twenty or thirty years, during which time they have had five or six Morgans. It is all very cosy.

Morgan has a unique niche in the market, but I am surprised to find that the company has absolutely no idea what the demand for the car is. It seems to think that it is no higher than 500 cars a year, but if the car starts to sell in the United States, I believe it might even be as high as 1000.

There is no computer in the stockroom and Bill Warwin who is in charge of the operation simply re-orders when stocks of a particular item look low. The stockroom not only services the factory, it also supplies spare parts to Morgan owners. Several thousand items are stocked and the number is constantly growing. Historically Morgan has held high levels of stock as a buffer against industrial problems at their suppliers, especially in those situations where the company has only one supplier.

Bill Warwin tells me the average stock level is between three and four months' supply. But no one is sitting down and working out what the optimum level of stock ought to be. I am almost certain that stock levels are higher than they need to be with the result that the company has far too much money tied up in stock.

Maurice Owen, the chief development engineer, is not the youngest member of the Morgan management team. He also suffers from arthritis. But in spite of these handicaps he is one of the few people working at Morgan with any clear sense of what is wrong with the company and any sort of vision of what it could become.

The design philosophy behind Morgan is to redefine and improve the mechanics while maintaining the shape of the body. The last four or five years have been spent adapting the mechanics of the car to meet new legislation. The car now has dual braking and the emphasis of current work is on the use of unleaded fuels.

Morgan drivers, those who are fanatical about the car, are a conservative lot and have a reputation for disliking changes to the car. I wondered how difficult it was for Maurice to introduce change. The problem of Morgan's hard ride and what to do about it is very much in the air at the moment. Maurice is looking at the possibility of introducing a new suspension system, but would Morgan owners wear it; or do they relish that famous bumpy ride?

According to Maurice Owen, worrying about the reaction of Morgan owners can be a big restraint on management thinking. Apparently it took him eleven or twelve years to persuade the company to go over to rack and pinion steering which now makes the car very firm and responsive to drive.

Maurice Owen thinks the way the car is made is wrong. He likens it to making prototypes. He would like to see the car made in different units. At the moment the engines are put on the chassis at the beginning, the bodywork is then fitted on to the chassis, and the wiring is put in last. On one model, this last operation involves the fitters in wild contortions to get the wiring in place.

Maurice Owen is convinced the factory could be better

organised. He would like to build the body and chassis separately. The body could be sprayed and even wired and the engine wouldn't need to be put in until the end, avoiding the current situation whereby expensive engines sit around on the chassis for three or four months while the cars are completed.

He points to the fact that although all the different Morgan models look basically the same, they aren't – they all have a slightly different chassis or bodywork. Maurice Owen sees no reason why Morgan cannot retain a range of models but iron out the small, insignificant differences which make the production of the car so inefficient. He would like all the cars to have the same chassis and the same basic body. Apparently he has been saying this for years, and he is still working on the problem, however, as he puts it himself, he feels he would be drummed out of the Brownies if he mentioned it again. Whenever the subject is mentioned the instant reaction is always the same: the customers like the car made the way it is, and it is this antiquated way of doing things that actually sells the car. As he says, it's a crazy way to run a business.

Maurice Owen confirmed most of my first impressions of the factory and the way Morgans are made. The ethos of the company is very risk averse, except that they seem to have no idea they are actually steering the most risky course of all when they fail to face up to change.

I end my day rather more worried than when I began. My initial reaction is that the mild solutions they propose are not going to be enough to preserve them in the long run and I think the idea of doing anything radical is very difficult for them to accept.

Everyone at Morgan believes the success of the car is due to the way it's traditionally built. There's an enormous in-built desire to hang on to the old methods. But in the long term I think they are doomed because these production methods will become too expensive. With the notable exception of their chief development engineer, Maurice Owen, everyone I met appears to have set their face against change. The business is just a little too comfortable at the moment, so there appears to be no immediate need to face up to change.

Complacency is a big problem. From their point of view they are doing so well at the moment that they can see no need to change and none of them are really aware of the dangers they face. I'm rather doubtful about my ability to convince them that the dangers are real and that the need for change is urgent.

When you go round the factory, there's hardly a shop which couldn't do with new investment: Morgan seems dedicated to making things in the most expensive way, and this really can't bode well for the future. Everybody defends their own corner and there is this iron-strong belief that any change of any sort will in some magical way alter the attraction of the car and the whole house of cards will come tumbling down.

However, my visit convinces me that the company is in real peril unless it can accept the need for change. They may enjoy what they are doing, but the company is run in a totally unbusinesslike way. There are so many ways production and profitability could be improved, but they all involve making big changes.

I am as convinced as ever that the choices are quite stark. Now I have seen the factory I am even firmer in my view that the management must find some way of getting their workforce to produce more cars. If they don't they will find themselves priced out of the market by labour costs, which will go on accounting for an ever-increasing proportion of the cost of making the car.

Morgan has the potential to be a very successful company. But the management must want to tackle the problem of their waiting list which is absolutely fundamental to the company's malaise. I want Morgan out there in the market place feeling confident about its future and its product. If people can make money trading their position on the Morgan waiting list there is clearly scope for increasing the price of the car, and I for one would like to see Morgan place itself in a slightly higher price bracket.

The waiting list protects Morgan from having to actually go out and sell its wares. It must find out how many cars it could sell and must then set about satisfying the demand. I don't know what that demand is, but I'm sure it is more than the 500 cars a year it intends making if it succeeds in increasing its production from nine to ten cars a week.

If it is, this clearly has major implications for the way the car is made. I want the Morgan management to look at the reality of the situation. At the moment they play at being businessmen. If Morgan is to become a serious business and if it is to make the transition from a company that is production led to one driven by demand for its product, then it must face up to the need for change. If it is to satisfy demand, Morgan needs a major investment programme to increase efficiency, and this means introducing an element of automation.

The recent incremental approach of trying to increase production by one car a week and then another car a week is not, I think, going to get Morgan very far. I agree that the hand-built nature of the car must be preserved, and it is also important to preserve the wide range of options that are available on the car. I am sure it is a real marketing advantage to be able to have a choice of fittings, and to have the car and the upholstery almost any colour one likes. These are sensible things to have. Morgan also believes there are good engineering reasons for having wooden body frames, and I wouldn't quarrel with that. I just don't share Morgan's belief that its customers will make for the door if it introduces a limited amount of automation.

The factory is very badly organised even for the way the car is made at the moment, the material flow through the factory is chaotic, and a ludicrous amount of time is wasted. Morgan say the bottleneck is in the sheet metal shop and if this is the case there is really no option but to change the whole method of manufacturing the car. They claim it takes four years to train someone to work in the metal shop, so, in theory, nothing can happen for four years unless they make some changes to working methods. I just cannot believe that the difference between hand-beating a panel completely, and pressing it into its basic shape and then hand-finishing it, is going to alter anyone's decision to buy this car.

If Morgan decides to do nothing, I'm sure that everybody will go on being very happy for a while. They will remember my visit with a certain wry humour. But over a period of time the Morgan will disappear. I don't know how long it'll be, it may be ten years, it may be fifteen, but I think it will disappear.

I would feel very sad if this car went. The company is still financially strong enough to tackle change. It has a very popular car, a vast order book and a number of further developments in the pipeline. If it wanted it could go public and raise enough money to totally re-equip the factory. But all this requires a lot of determination and I'm not sure anybody at Morgan really sees it my way.

Peter and Charles and I meet a couple of days later to

discuss my initial impressions. Peter Morgan has now run the company for thirty years ever since his father died in 1959. The odds in favour of a company like Morgan surviving were slender. Peter Morgan's monument is the continuing survival of Morgan. His achievement is the remarkable reputation of the car and its dedicated band of loyal followers. His style of management is best characterised as cautious. The long Morgan waiting list is his insurance policy against hard times. The antiquated production methods are defended with the argument that much of the Morgan mystique rests on the fact that the Morgan is hand-built and this magic would somehow evaporate with any modification to the time-honoured way in which Morgans have been built for the last fifty years.

Charles is Peter's obvious heir apparent, and in early 1989 it was Peter Morgan's intention to retire on reaching 70 in November and hand over the reins to Charles.

Charles is more ambitious for the company. He wants to capitalise on the obvious demand for the car, and he wants the company to make more money. He thinks the company capable of doubling in size, and has plans to introduce air tools and computerised stock control. He wants more research and development, including a new suspension system to correct the Morgan's notoriously bumpy ride. He has even thought about marketing Morgan accessories, such as ties and leather goods.

But Charles is also quite diffident. He has only been with the company for three years and I get the impression he is still feeling his way. None the less, the car and the factory are almost literally in his blood. As a younger man he followed in his father's footsteps and raced a works model, doing reasonably well against cars such as the Porsche 911 SP Turbo. Charles clearly has a lot of respect for his father and his achievements, but changing the factory may mean that at some stage he will have to confront his father. It gives his views a certain ambivalence and lack of decisiveness, and like Peter, there are times when Charles also clings to the old time-honoured ways of doing things.

Charles sees Morgan facing various dilemmas. He thinks the company could be more thrusting and economically successful with more modern manufacturing methods, but he also thinks there is value in the old methods and the level of service they offer their customers. He says the size of the waiting list obviously shows they aren't making enough Morgans, but on the other hand he also feels quite proud of the waiting list. He knows they need to computerise their spares department, but is worried that this would entail abandoning the personal contact.

He doesn't seem to have understood that solving problems like these is what the job of management is all about. However, his biggest problem is getting his father to accept change. Peter is fond of quoting the head of the Porsche car company who is reputed to have said that fathers found businesses, which are consolidated by their sons and then ruined by their grandsons. It is Charles' fear that there may be more than a grain of truth in Herr Porsche's view of the progress of family firms.

In retrospect I think Peter and Charles are quite shocked by my criticisms of the factory. I get the feeling they had expected me to endorse their methods, and come up with a few practical tips which they could easily implement for increasing production to ten cars a week. I am sure my criticisms rattle them. From then on I think they both feel under siege, and are unable to appreciate how enthusiastic I am about the Morgan car and my real desire to get the company to the position where it is really motoring and fulfilling its potential.

I tell them that I don't look on the very long order book as a sign of health. Quite the reverse: I see it as a potential danger. No one could tell me what the sustainable demand for the car is. I am given all sorts of numbers by Derek Day, the sales director, but they are basically meaningless. I tell them they need to get a better idea of what the demand is. Everybody believes they can make 500 cars a year, but I am not sure this will do a great deal to reduce the waiting time.

At the moment we know that a quite high proportion of people on the waiting list cancel their order at some time during their wait. But nobody can tell me why, or whether the fall-off rate is a reflection of current demand. Does the fall-off rate decline when orders decline or the other way round, or is there no correlation?

I am sure that Peter Morgan is correct when he says that if the waiting list was wiped out overnight, you couldn't assume a consistent level of demand. The demand is cyclical. But that's just Peter Morgan's hunch; the company hasn't actually got any figures to back this up.

At the time of my first visit, Morgan were going for class approval in the United States. Until they get it, Morgans can only be supplied in the United States if they are converted to run on propane. However, if the company gets approval for their new clean-burn engine the car can go on sale in the United States without modification, and demand for the car on the other side of the Atlantic could be hard to satisfy.

Morgan has a keen and loyal workforce. It's the biggest collective love affair I've ever seen. Everybody loves the car, loves the factory, loves the business. There is a passion about the car which is wonderful to see and a great strength. But then there is the flipside: I have never been anywhere where there is such total conservatism with a little 'c'. I think introducing change here is going to be real blood, sweat and tears.

I explain that my preliminary diagnosis indicates that change is going to be such a hell of a battle that they might as well go for a radical solution to their problems. I tell them I am alarmed about the lack of flexibility. The way they do things now, the pressure point is always likely to be the sheet-metal shop. They can't buy in extra people and the training period is so long that they have a three- or four-year lead time before they can do anything about that particular bottleneck.

Peter Morgan is concerned that the size of the factory is a physical constraint on expansion. I am not convinced that this is the case. I don't think space is a major limiting factor.

A couple of weeks later Peter, Charles and I meet again over lunch. I hope to persuade them to take a fundamental look at their business and that they should at least look at what substantial change might involve. If they do, then I think the Morgan could go on for a great many years. It is not a greedy business and we are not talking about an enormous output. The company has only ever built 30 000 or so Morgans, so they aren't trying to compete with the likes of Toyota.

There are some complicated psychological factors at work, and I have to find a way to make it safe for Peter to allow Charles to move ahead. At this stage I am convinced that Charles is probably more willing to change than Peter. In fact it is Charles who takes up a very defensive position. He feels I have failed to appreciate his father's achievements in bringing the company through some very difficult times, and in adapting to legislation which all but killed the sports car.

In spite of their long waiting list, Peter is still terrified that demand for the car could simply evaporate overnight. His memory of empty order books, even though this is now over twenty years ago, is still very strong. There is a basic lack of confidence in the demand for the car, and in themselves as managers.

I explain that if they updated their production methods, not only would they be able to make more cars with the same workforce, on the same premises, but they would also have a more flexible way of working which could expand and contract if demand did fluctuate. I have some ideas on how they could do this, but when I suggest discussing them, I meet a brick wall of resistance.

I get the impression that they think I only see things in black and white, so I try to make it quite clear that what worries me is that here is a company which is not realising its potential, and which if it continues to resist change puts its business at very considerable risk.

Charles thinks I am making a mistake when I reject their incremental approach to increasing production. As we are talking Morgan is struggling to squeeze a further one car a week out of its workforce to bring production up from nine to ten cars a week. However, on further investigation it becomes clear that any idea of upping the numbers of cars produced each week, in stages, one a year, is not something that anyone has talked about. It would involve taking on extra trainees and there are no current plans to do that.

I suggest they might like to get together with their own production engineer, Maurice Owen, and an outside consultant, to take a fundamental look at the way the car is now made, and to explore whether it could be made more economically than at present without losing its hand-made image.

I am only asking them to investigate the possibility of

change, I am not asking them to actually do it. But it becomes increasingly clear that the idea of change, let alone the need for change, is something that both Peter and Charles find very difficult to cope with. Both prevaricate: Charles by denying that they are against change, Peter by using the excuse that they have thought about it before but somehow it never comes about, because it is all too difficult.

I don't blame them for being bound up in the day-to-day problems of management, but I don't get the impression that they have sat down together to discuss my criticisms ahead of today's meeting. The bonds between the two are clearly very strong, but I get the impression that neither wants to upset the other with ideas which might lead to tension between them. There is no management consensus on how the company should progress. And to be fair to them, before I arrived on the scene to challenge all their preconceived notions, they probably didn't see the necessity of any kind of long-term management plan. At one point Peter says he never looks further than five years ahead.

My points are continually evaded, and because there is no sense of urgency about the place, no one actually feels the need for change deep down in their bones where it really matters. At one point Peter discusses the possibility of Morgan losing its independence and it almost appears that he would prefer his company to be gobbled up by some entrepreneur rather than have to implement radical changes himself.

Charles sidetracks the issues by bringing up his idea of using the Morgan logo to merchandise a range of luxury goods. I am not necessarily against the idea, although I do think it is peripheral. To my mind Morgan's business is making motor cars and until they have realised the potential of the business they already have, worrying about marketing other merchandise is a waste of management resources.

They both say they want to do something about the waiting list, but I have to keep on pointing out to them that their present plan to increase production by 40 cars a year is not going to have much effect. They really need a much more vigorous approach to the problem.

No one would ever call my approach indirect, and yet I find I am having a great deal of difficulty getting Peter and Charles to understand and take on board what I am saying.

I have one last go at setting out the three areas of Morgan's business which cause me concern, including the one area where they should make a start by hiring a consultant.

They need to think about the demand for the car. No one knows how many cars they could sell if there were only a short waiting list, or what will happen to demand if the United States market opens up to them. They also need to think about the high level of stock they have tied up in their operation. And finally, and most importantly, they need to take a long hard look at the way the car is made, and to help them do this they should hire a consultant to show them how the most modern technology could contribute to their operation.

I point out that Morgan is in the enviable position of being able to afford change. This is almost the exact opposite of what I often find when I visit companies: most are anxious to expand but lack the financial resources to do so. Morgan isn't in this particular dilemma. It is currently making a profit, and if it couldn't generate enough from its own operations and from bank borrowings, it would have no trouble raising money if it went public and sold some of its shares.

By the end of the lunch I manage to persuade Charles that it would be worth at least considering my proposals, and that it would be a good idea if Peter, Charles and Maurice Owen, their chief development engineer, could work as a small group with the help of an outside consultant to advise them on modern production methods. I am not sure if I manage to win over Peter.

And so it turns out. During the summer, the television crew returns to film a Morgan rally in Scotland. Peter Morgan is present and is asked to comment on my visit. It is as if I had never been there. Peter emphasises all the good things I said about the company: a fine car, all the optional extras, and their devoted followers, while totally ignoring all my criticisms. Any idea that they might form a small management group, and bring in an outside consultant, has been shelved.

I care passionately about Morgan, and I find it very difficult to accept that my proposals, which seem the very essence of good sense, should fall on such deaf ears. I want to take the management and give them a good shake. I find it almost unbearable to see a company with such potential literally going to waste.

I write to Peter Morgan offering my assistance in setting up a series of meetings with the production engineer who I feel would be able to help Morgan plan a more efficient factory. My offers are all met with polite refusals.

As a last resort I ask if we could have one last meeting and am delighted when they agree to see me towards the end of November. This is my last chance to really find out whether the gospel of change which I have been preaching has in any way influenced the way Peter and Charles are thinking.

In the six months since my last visit, Morgan has moved

that much closer to being able to sell its cars in the United States without having them converted to run on propane. If the new clean-burn engine passes US emission tests, Morgan can sell its cars in the United States for the next two years, during which time it must develop a better restraint system: either one which prevents the car being started unless the seat belts are attached, or an air bag.

The prospect of a massive surge of orders from the United States, plus very strong orders from their traditional markets, has galvanised Charles into action. He is not being as bold and as brave as I would like, but I am very pleased to see that he is now openly discussing the problems of how to increase production with his father. They disagree about which is the best way forward, but at least they are talking.

I am delighted to find that Charles has taken it upon himself to find out more about modern manufacturing techniques. He has enrolled for an evening course at Worcester Technical College which will involve visits to some technically advanced factories.

As I predicted, the experiment to increase production from nine to ten cars a week lasted not much longer than the three-week trial. However, Charles is now working with Maurice Owen on a plan to increase production by a quarter. This would involve a number of changes to the layout and sequence of production, changes which he believes could be implemented during the factory's summer closure in 1990.

In spite of the earlier failure to increase production from nine to ten cars a week, Peter is still talking about increasing production incrementally, so even if Charles does develop a workable plan, he will still need to persuade his father that his way is the best way forward.

There is no doubt that Peter is finding the idea of retirement very difficult. And perhaps I don't find this so hard to understand. He has run the company now, through thick and thin, for thirty years, and it has been part of his life since he was a small boy. Letting go of something which is such a central part of your existence must be difficult.

Peter always said he would retire on his seventieth birthday at the beginning of November. And so he did, at least on paper. On the Friday following his birthday there was a little party, and the shopfloor presented him with a surprise magnum of champagne. On the following Monday, he was back at his desk.

For the time being at least Peter remains firmly in control whatever the words on his pension book say. He stays on as chairman, although he has decided to call himself chief executive rather than managing director which possibly indicates a desire to step aside from the day-to-day problems of management. Charles is definitely second in command although there are no current plans to promote him beyond his current position of production director.

I have been involved with Morgan for less than a year, but even I am having difficulty letting go. What are my final impressions? I am so conditioned by my low expectations that I am grateful for almost any change that is proposed in this most conservative of all factories. After my last visit I believed they would make no changes of any sort. Now I think they will make some.

There are definite signs that Charles is becoming more assertive and more effective, and although Peter's retirement has turned out to be nominal rather than actual, I do feel he is pulling back a little and giving Charles greater freedom to operate.

I still fail to see why they won't put up the price of the

cars. It would be the quickest way of reducing the waiting list and it would increase profits, which could then be used to increase the efficiency of the factory; both extremely desirable aims. However, they cling to the idea that they have a mission in life to provide cars at a certain price to a certain type of person whom they happen to like. This kind of thinking is a sentence of death for any business.

Are the changes they are now tentatively contemplating going to be enough to secure the long-term future of Morgan into the next century? On the present evidence, I somehow doubt it. But any change is better than no change at all. And who knows, if they find they can make moderate changes with good effect, they might possibly develop a taste for it.

5

Shropshire District Health Authority

Shropshire District Health Authority administers the National Health Service in the area covered by the whole county of Shropshire. It covers more than 1300 square miles and stretches from Whitchurch in the north to Ludlow in the south, a distance of 50 miles. It serves a population of just over 400 000 nearly half of whom live in the county town of Shrewsbury or the new and expanding town of Telford.

At the time of my first visit in March 1989, Shropshire was facing a budget crisis. It had overspent its last two years' budgets and was having to make cuts of £2 million to its 1989–90 budget. If the worst happens and the members fail to agree the cuts, the government has the power to disband the authority and appoint a commissioner to run it. This point hasn't been reached yet, but the authority's future independence is finely balanced.

Ken Morris's official title is district general manager. He is Shropshire's chief administrator. In October 1988, he prepared a package of expenditure cuts aimed at balancing the budget. The cuts must be agreed at the authority's March 1989 meeting if they are to meet the deadline for setting a legal budget, and there are rumblings that his proposals are in danger of being thrown out by the authority's members.

These are pressing issues and they must be resolved in the next couple of weeks. My involvement with Shropshire is intended to last several months. Ken is interested in my advice on the authority's long-term strategy for delivering health care to the people of Shropshire, an area with a growing and, like everywhere else, an ageing population.

In 1988 I was one of the judges of the *Sunday Times* 'Best of Health' competition. I became fascinated by the problems of managing a public authority responsible for providing something as vital as health care within what is to all intents and purposes a fixed budget. I had always wondered how well the National Health Service is managed but I hadn't realised how complex and difficult the problems are.

There are many similarities between running a business and running a public authority, but there are also some crucial differences. Judging that competition taught me that the quality of the service was very largely determined by the quality of the management. This was the one crucial factor. It was more important even than the amount of money there was to spend.

Just as in business, one of the main functions of a health service manager is to drive down costs so that services can be delivered as efficiently as possible. But quite unlike most businesses, the health service doesn't need to market its services, except when it chooses to for reasons of public health. The demand is always there; not only that, it appears to be growing like Topsy.

Demand ends up being rationed. Some of it is obvious, such as waiting lists for operations; some of it more subtle, like long waiting times in GPs' surgeries which deter people from consulting their GP unless they are at death's door. Strangely, one of the few businesses which shares this characteristic with the health service is the Morgan Motor Company, a company I visited in this series.

All managers must develop political skills, in the broadest sense. Much of management is dealing with people, persuading them, cajoling them, motivating them. The best-run companies are those which have a clearly developed ethos which is understood, shared and owned by everyone. Even in the best of possible worlds, conflicts and tensions arise, but good managers know how to use conflict creatively to bring about change.

But this is nothing to the political skills a health service manager needs to operate. No business is required to sell its goods and services to everyone, but the health service must provide a universal service available to every man, woman and child in the country. Even those people who opt for private medicine end up in an NHS ambulance and hospital if they crash their car on the motorway.

The government channels money into the health service through twenty-four English and Welsh regional health authorities who then have the job of deciding how much each district health authority should get.

Shropshire District Health Authority has nineteen members, who are drawn from a variety of sources. The chairman, Frank Jones, who is paid a small salary, is appointed by the Secretary of State.

The regional health authority is responsible for appointing the majority of the members – eleven in all. By tradition one of these is a nurse and another a GP, although the majority are political appointments. Two members are nominated by Shropshire County Council, another four from the various district councils: these six members are all local councillors.

The political appointments are carved up by the political

parties in proportion to their strength on the local authorities within the area. In Shropshire, roughly two-thirds of the political appointees are Conservatives, the remainder being drawn from the other parties. And lastly, there is a medical academic appointed by Birmingham University.

Shropshire District Health Authority falls within the West Midlands region, and competes with twenty-two other areas for its money.

We all have our opinion of the health service and how it should be run. Health service managers cannot expect an easy ride when the strategies they so carefully work out, and so carefully cost, actually involve radical changes to the way that service is provided.

They must develop an extraordinary talent for selling their ideas, their vision. Their first task is to sell it to the public because only then will they be able to sell it to the members of the health authority, many of whom represent local interests or dogmatic political views. It is not an enviable task, but the health service managers who can pick their way through this minefield will have developed skills that many private-sector managers would envy.

The strategy Ken Morris has devised for Shropshire has been controversial. The authority started out with at least twenty hospitals and 2300 beds. It has decided to concentrate most of its hospital activities into two hospitals: the brand new, and at the time of my first visit only partially opened, Princess Royal Hospital at Telford, and the much older Royal Shrewsbury, at Shrewsbury, which is badly in need of modernisation.

The problems have arisen because the money to run the new hospital in Telford and to make other savings is to come from the closure of ten smaller hospitals. The policy has been immensely unpopular. Highly successful local campaigns to save the hospitals have sprung up, attracting a lot of local press, radio and TV coverage. Some have even succeeded in delaying the closure of their hospital. By March 1989, Ken has won agreement to close six of the ten smaller hospitals.

And as if this wasn't enough for Shropshire District Health Authority to cope with, the government then adds a further complication with the publication of its White Paper on the Health Service. It is the most radical rethink of the National Health Service since it was set up in 1948. As well as allowing hospitals to opt out of district health authority control it is also intended to completely alter the relationship of GPs and hospitals. Demand for hospital services is created in large part not by patients but by the GPs who refer them. The White Paper wants GPs to be aware of the cost of referral. The idea is to give GPs budgets and the freedom to shop around for the best-value hospital services.

It is against this background that I become involved with Shropshire. Ken's office has absolutely inundated me with facts, figures and papers. There doesn't seem to be any shortage of data about the NHS, but I have rarely found data so badly digested. It's all too easy to get buried under a mountain of statistics.

My fear is that this can be a serious deterrent to clear thinking and the ability to get quickly and easily to the real issues. I get the feeling that burying himself under a pile of paper is one of Ken's best defences against the obvious stresses of his job.

At our first meeting Ken explains his strategy for Shropshire; in spite of all the problems he has encountered, he is still resolutely committed to closing the smaller hospitals. In his view, Ken is modernising the provision of health care in Shropshire. By concentrating hospital activities in two centres of excellence, he expects to transform Shropshire's NHS from a low-technology, low-throughput operation to one characterised by high technology and high capital investment.

He points to the fact that the NHS is no longer expected to offer a comprehensive service, and that there is a growing trend for the burden of the so-called 'Cinderella services', the long-term care of the old and mentally ill, to be shared between the NHS, the local authorities, voluntary and private sectors. He sees his failure to persuade the public of the need for these changes as nothing more than a breakdown in public relations. He appears confident about his policy, and I am left somewhat puzzled as to why he felt he needed my advice.

I, on the other hand, have questions of my own which I want answering. For example, I am extremely worried by the size of the waiting list. If there is one measure of the efficiency of a local health authority, it is the speed with which it delivers its service to the public. Shropshire has one of the longest waiting lists in the country. There are over 8000 people waiting for operations, and a third have waited more than a year.

Ken seems to be of the view that non-urgent operations can, and perhaps even should, wait indefinitely. I find this view exceedingly cynical. Looking at it from the patients' point of view, there are 8000 people in Shropshire who have been told by their doctors that they need an operation. It creates expectation, and if that expectation isn't fulfilled it inevitably breeds dissatisfaction. Patients have been told they need these operations and it matters to them whether they have it this year, next year, some time, never. It really is preposterous to suggest otherwise.

I now need to learn more about the way Shropshire delivers health care at the grass roots. I start my fact-finding mission by visiting a cottage hospital at Much Wenlock, and the Beeches, a long-stay hospital for the elderly, both of which have been threatened with closure.

What I find is a revelation. Here are two hospitals who know the value of the service they offer their local community, and who are determined to stay open. Staff, who ten years ago had no concerns beyond their roles as carers, have suddenly discovered all manner of latent entrepreneurial talents.

After seeing the work at Much Wenlock I have real doubts about Ken's policy of shutting down a lot of cottage hospitals. It seems certain that cases which used to be dealt with at small hospitals like Much Wenlock will simply get pushed on to one of the two large county hospitals where they are bound to cost more, and which will be less convenient for the patients.

I am surprised by the buzz of ideas surrounding the place. The hospital wants to continue providing a service to local people, and to solve its funding problems it is exploring, completely off its own bat, ways in which it could raise additional money. The staff are talking about letting the second floor to Nuffield, the private hospital group. And there is the idea of getting a developer to build some sheltered housing in the very lovely hospital grounds, where the hospital could provide nursing care.

Over in Ironbridge at the Beeches, a long-stay hospital for the elderly, bed numbers have been cut from 119 to 63 in the previous year. The latest news is that the numbers of elderly must be cut further, to just 35. A ward is being painted to receive a similar number of elderly mentally ill patients from a larger psychiatric hospital. But Jacqui Harris, the manager, says they never know from one day to the next what to expect. Today the plan is to take in elderly psychiatric patients, tomorrow it could well be something else.

All she knows for sure is that she is going to end up with one hospital block boarded up and empty. With more and more elderly and disabled people being cared for at home, Jacqui Harris says, there is a demand for a short-stay home, with proper nursing care, where patients can come for a week or so to give their relatives a break. Local councils are paying thousands of pounds to private nursing homes for this kind of service. Mrs Harris is now working on a proposal to use the Beeches' redundant block as a short-stay nursing home, with the majority of the fees coming from the surrounding local councils.

I think it is important for the future of the health service that the medical staff should be as involved as possible in its management. They are the people who create the demand and who are ultimately responsible for the quality of care we all receive, and unless there is some sort of feedback which allows them to contribute to the overall strategy, they will inevitably feel they are working in a vacuum. Otherwise, everyone fights for their own corner and those with the loudest voices or the most glamorous speciality end up getting more than their share of available funds.

Bob Wilson combines the jobs of consultant physician and unit manager at the Royal Shrewsbury Hospital. With Bob as my guide, I toured the hospital talking to hospital doctors, visiting GPs, nursing staff and patients.

The Royal Shrewsbury Hospital has 900 beds. Although it is Shropshire's largest hospital, no one would ever describe it as efficient. It has grown over the years in a chaotic and piecemeal fashion. The buildings spread over two sites on either side of a main road, and part of it is based in old army huts left over from the Second World War. It's a management nightmare; expensive to run as well as badly in need of some rationalisation and rebuilding. Telford Hospital, the county's other major hospital, which completed its phased opening in August 1989, has only 385 beds.

I want to know what the medical staff think they can do to reduce the waiting lists, and where the actual bottleneck is occurring. Is it a shortage of medical staff, is it a shortage of operating theatres, or is it a lack of beds?

No one is in any doubt where the fault lies. According to Bob Wilson there just aren't enough beds to go round. Most days medical admissions spill over into the surgical wards, and operations have to be cancelled. Bob Wilson knows it's inexcusable that in one month alone they telephoned 135 patients on the day they were due to come in, cancelling their operations.

I know the waiting list should theoretically be eased somewhat once the new hospital at Telford is opened. But this on its own won't clear the backlog. What will is beds, so I continue to be totally bemused as to why the authority seems so determined to shut down beds in the smaller hospitals. I see no reason why these beds shouldn't be used for longer-stay and post-operative patients, so freeing beds at Shrewsbury and, when it is open, Telford. I would like to see the authority explore some of the mixed-economy solutions being proposed by the staff I have met at these smaller hospitals.

I know there is always this question of money, and I am sure the National Health Service deserves more. It means that at Shropshire, and I am sure in many other places too, the service is driven not by the needs of the patients, but by the need to save money. This is a very negative way to run anything, and although everywhere I go I meet smiling, dedicated people, I do sense that morale is very low.

I am also worried by the apparent policy of shifting a proportion of the authority's costs on to other organisations such as social security and local authority social services departments. By closing the cottage hospitals the health authority is effectively washing its hands of responsibility for long-stay, mainly elderly, patients. I know this is government policy, but there is precious little evidence that the local authorities are providing adequate family support services, or that social security can continue to meet the cost of private nursing homes. It sounds like pass the parcel to me, and the parcel in this case is people.

I would like to see Shropshire's managers take an imaginative leap and turn their management problems on their head. They need to start again. I am sure that when the present strategy was planned ten years ago the aim was to provide what they believed to be the best service for the people of Shropshire. But that strategy has now been completely hijacked by the need to make cuts. None of the medical staff feel they understood the strategy. All they see is muddle, and what a lot of people describe as 'constantly moving goal posts'.

And yet the managers I meet are still convinced that they have the best of all possible strategies and that it is just the stupidity and intransigence of everyone else which is preventing them from implementing it. It's as if they are operating in a vacuum on some planet which has been swept clean of any untidy consumers, or noisy councillors. When asked how they intend selling their policies to the public, they have no ideas.

Managing a health authority is a highly complex business. The more complicated the management problems, the more there is a need for a simple, clear statement of strategy which is first and foremost achievable and acceptable but which is also comprehensible and capable of being communicated to everyone who works in the organisation and, in the case of a health authority, to the public as well.

Instead of being finance led, they must go back to first principles and start thinking about what the customer wants – what services do we need to provide for the people of Shropshire, how are we going to do it within our budget, and what will our priorities be? I want the managers to work alongside the professionals as they develop this new strategy.

At the moment the thrust of management is negative; it is aimed at stopping people doing things. Approaching the problem from the needs of the customer frees management to think more positively, more imaginatively. It was this approach which made it possible for Brighton District Health Authority to launch its cataract fortnight in 1988. By setting up the kind of cataract operation conveyor belt more commonly seen in the Third World, they cleared their waiting list for this simple, but life-enhancing, operation in just two weeks.

Frank Jones is Shropshire District Health Authority's chairman. This is where the buck stops. Frank Jones is the man responsible for the efficient planning and delivery of the county's health care, and I want to learn from the horse's mouth how he tackles this enormously difficult and complex task.

District Health Authority chairmen are appointed by the Secretary of State for a period of five years. When I meet him, Frank has just over a year left to run, and if he is judged a success he can expect to be appointed for a further five years. On paper at least, his credentials – an entrepreneur with enthusiasm and a dedication to public works – tailor-make him for a job such as this. Frank retired in 1984, at the relatively young age of fifty-five, after he sold the highly successful food company he had built from scratch over the previous twenty years.

Frank lives in some style in an impressive Georgian house in the centre of Shrewsbury, and this is where we agree to meet. Obviously a man of action, I can't imagine him happily seeing out his days on the golf course, or dead-heading the roses in his garden. Instead he busies himself with public works. Shropshire District Health Authority is not his only job; he also finds time to chair Telford's Development Corporation.

I get the impression that Frank doesn't find much satisfaction running Shropshire's health authority. As an entrepreneur, I am not sure how well he has adapted to the more purely managerial culture of a health authority. Entrepreneurs like Frank who build their own companies don't work through committees, they don't need to delicately pick their way through, and then pull together, the views of a wide variety of different interest groups, nor do they necessarily have to develop finely tuned political antennae. They are much more used to a world where what they say goes.

Frank doesn't appear particularly worried about Shropshire's future. I was hoping to find him brimming over with fresh ideas for solving the county's problems. Instead he seems demoralised and worn down by the whole process.

It looks as if he has run out of steam. All he can see is the negative side of the job: how the government fails to fund pay increases, how difficult it is to get anyone to agree to anything. He believes he is shut in by the political environment and powerless to do anything about it. If the chairman, the man who is meant to be leading by his vision, lacks a sense of direction, no wonder the rest of the authority feels as if it is drifting nowhere. I really believe that Frank has lost the initiative.

My opinion is confirmed by the budget drama which reaches its final denouement at the authority's March meeting. Ken's programme of cuts, in their various forms, has been on the table since October, but instead of passing them on the nod, a group of members led by Peter Dunham presents the meeting with an alternative set of cuts which they believe are likely to be more broadly acceptable to the authority's members.

It appears that Ken's cuts were unlikely to get sufficient support from the members and might possibly have been thrown out, so the authority would have found themselves unable to set a legal budget. The impetus for the alternative proposals comes from this group, led by Peter Dunham, who aren't prepared to risk this and have gone ahead and prepared their own budget.

I don't carry any particular torch for what has become known as the Dunham package – in fact it bears the hallmark of being cobbled together. But the whole ramshackle way in which Shropshire finally set their 1989–90 budget demonstrates both Ken Harris's inability to sell his management's proposals to the members of the authority and just how out of touch, and out of sympathy, he is with them. And of course the one is a symptom of the other; together they add up to lack of effective leadership and loss of initiative.

I now think it is time for me to find out how Shropshire's

problems are seen from the top. The county's paymaster is the West Midlands Regional Health Authority, an area which covers 5.5 million people, has 102 000 employees and for management purposes is divided into 22 districts. I arrange to meet the chairman, businessman Sir James Ackers at Walford Hall, a country club near Stratford.

I learn a lot about Sir James's style of management. He clearly likes to leave his district health authorities to work out their own problems: if they dig themselves into holes, he thinks it is their job to dig themselves out again. He manages by the carrot and stick method. He strikes bargains with his district authorities. If they do something for him, he will do something for them, which usually means giving them money.

Even though Telford is only 15 miles from Shrewsbury, it was decided that a town growing as fast as Telford needed its own hospital. In 1984 Sir James Ackers struck a bargain with Shropshire: if the county could find savings worth half the running costs of the new hospital at Telford, the region would finance the other half.

Sir James is sympathetic to the problems of Shropshire, but is also critical of the management. I agree with him that big rural counties must be difficult to manage, and Shropshire has the added difficulty of a fast-growing new town clamouring for its share of available resources, which creates a tension between the old Shropshire which looks towards Shrewsbury and the newcomers who naturally gravitate to Telford.

It is Sir James's view that Shropshire, with more than twenty hospitals, had more than it needs, even for a large rural county, and that savings must inevitably come from closing some of the smaller hospitals.

I arrive on the scene as the county struggles to meet its side of the bargain, and all I can see is a policy in tatters. Nor is it one that I can support when I don't feel that some of the mixed-economy solutions put forward at the grass roots are being fully explored. What I fail to appreciate until my meeting with Sir James is how irritated he is by the cackhanded manner in which Shropshire has been implementing the closures.

Sir James Ackers understands the attachment that people in small country towns have for their local hospitals and that closing hospitals in rural areas is always going to be more difficult than in urban areas where the alternative hospital is still relatively easy to get to. Sir James is critical of the way Shropshire has handled the closures. He is convinced that success depends on having a clear, consistent plan: the health authority should decide which hospitals it is going to close and then stick to it.

Apparently Shropshire hasn't done this. Its hit list of hospitals due for closure is constantly changing, which he feels has brought nothing but confusion for both the authority and the people of Shropshire. He points to a neighbouring district which has managed to close five hospitals very skilfully, with hardly a word of protest.

Sir James has a poor opinion of the quality of Shropshire's financial management, which he says has a difficult time balancing its books. They don't control staff numbers carefully enough, and when they do rationalise, the estimated savings tend to come in lower than projected. Shropshire is in the habit of blaming the growing population, but according to Sir James other parts of the region with growing populations seem to manage to control costs. Of all the districts, Shropshire is the one which gives Sir

James Ackers the biggest headache. The saga of finding its share of the money to run the new Telford hospital has now gone on for five years, and is still unresolved.

I want to have Sir James Ackers's reaction to the idea of finding mixed-economy solutions as a way of keeping the smaller hospitals open. He seems so sure that closing the hospitals is the only way out of Shropshire's budgetary crisis that I wonder if he is receptive to such a suggestion.

In fact I find he is keen to explore the idea. It's news to me, but Shropshire has already put forward a mixed-economy solution for the cottage hospital at Broseley. The region has even said it supports the idea, and yet nothing happens. As Sir James says, it does seem that Shropshire finds it very difficult to make the kinds of decision which are common in business and, he adds, in other health district authorities as well.

I voice my concern about the size and length of the waiting list, only to discover that Shropshire could have done something about this. The region has a special allocation of money specifically earmarked to help the districts cut waiting lists. Unfortunately Shropshire at the time of my visit has failed to agree an effective programme for using this money, and so hasn't been given any.

In spite of all its troubles, Sir James says he is beginning to sense a new mood of realism among the members of the health authority. I think there has been an element of brinkmanship in Sir James's handling of the affair. He has allowed Shropshire to walk to the edge of the precipice in the hope that it wouldn't plunge into the abyss.

I suspect, although I wouldn't expect him to say so publicly, that Sir James shares my doubts about whether the existing management has the vision to abandon its old ways and take a radical look at where the county is going, and how it is managed. They need to formulate a plan which they believe they can carry out and which also involves and commands the support of the practitioners and the wider community, something they have singularly failed to do up until now.

If this meeting has achieved anything, I believe I may have reinforced Sir James's own suspicions and perhaps have helped persuade him that the situation is more urgent and requires faster action than he had envisaged.

It is now May 1989. Shropshire District Health Authority managers have met again to put the finishing touches to the Dunham package of cuts. With that behind them, there is time for me to sit down with Frank Jones and Ken Morris to discuss my concerns about the future management of the authority.

I know that Frank Jones in particular feels I have failed to understand the difficulties he faces getting the members of his authority to understand and accept the budgetary constraints under which they must operate.

By the same token I think Frank and Ken also fail to see that I approach their problems with some humility. This is one of the most difficult jobs I have looked at. I believe that managing the health service is a nearly impossible task, and even if you did manage it nearly perfectly, I still think the system needs more money.

Having seen the chaos of the Royal Shrewsbury Hospital, the crumbling fabric of the buildings, the superhuman efforts that people at the grass roots are making to save money, I don't think anyone could fail to be convinced that the National Health Service needs more money.

But as well as money it needs and deserves really top-flight managers. But it won't get them until it is prepared to pay them and give them a framework in which to operate.

I don't think Frank and Ken need me to tell them that they have lost the management initiative: they already know this. All the signs are there. The time to make decisions gets shorter, everything is increasingly done on the run, more and more distrust creeps in, more and more information is sought, more and more people question your every move.

What I am now about to suggest are ways of regaining that initiative, so that Shropshire can move forward in a positive mood thinking not about what it can't do, but what it can. I want them to see that their problems – the difficulty of implementing their strategy, the waiting list, and the political environment – are all inextricably linked, and that it is a mistake to look at each in isolation.

With 8000 people on the waiting list, almost everyone in Shropshire must know at least one person among their friends and family who is waiting for treatment or an operation. The authority is therefore seen as an inefficient provider of health care and this sense of unease feeds through and affects its ability to implement its strategy. And when the only constraint on doing more operations is not a lack of doctors, or nurses, or operating theatres, but a shortage of beds and when a major plank in the authority's policy is actually reducing the number of beds, I am not surprised they have met so much resistance both from their own members and from the public.

I am not in a position to question Shropshire's overall strategy, but I do want the authority to think about finding new uses for the smaller hospitals which will allow them to have a continuing role in serving their local communities, and which should help diffuse some of the opposition to their plans and to be available for the day when I am sure they will be needed. They are the 'cheapest' beds around.

As we have already seen, Shropshire is modernising its hospital service by concentrating resources on the county's two major hospitals, the Royal Shrewsbury and the new hospital at Telford. The Telford hospital is to be paid for by the closure of ten smaller hospitals. People in rural areas are attached to their smaller hospitals. I realise Shropshire can't afford to keep them all, but for the life of me I can't understand why some of the mixed-economy ideas put forward by the existing staff are not being pursued with more enthusiasm.

The authority is looking at the idea of independent trusts which would run the smaller hospitals as private nursing homes. Regional chairman Sir James Ackers has informally given the go-ahead for one at Broseley, but still nothing happens.

I want Frank and Ken to put some attack into these proposals. They need to put two or three of their best managers on to the project, setting them a relatively short timetable for getting one of these trusts, or something similar, up and running.

The idea is to continue the main function of the smaller hospitals – providing continuing care for the seriously ill and elderly – but in a different guise. Most patients' fees will be paid for by the Department of Social Security, just as in any other private nursing home.

I share Sir James Ackers's concern about the propriety of off-loading a proportion of the NHS budget on to the Social Security budget, but this is undoubtedly the direction in which government policy is pushing the health authorities. I assume the government knows what it is doing, and you can't blame the Health Service for taking advantage of the opportunity. However, in Shropshire I saw nothing which led me to believe that this change was being planned.

So how do Frank and Ken go about regaining the management initiative? My prescription is a mixture of practical advice, style and psychology.

First of all Frank and Ken are both so demoralised from their battles that they no longer expect to win. It's a vicious downward spiral. The less you expect to win, the less confident you appear, the less likely you are to win. The pair of them need to set a more confident tone. I am sure they could get their policies across to their members and to the public much more successfully if they cut down on the mountain of information their members have to plough through before each monthly meeting. Ken believes that it is the members who insist upon it. But I am convinced that not much of it gets read, and that the members would actually be much better informed about the authority's business if no paper ran to more than two or three pages and a couple of pie charts.

This may seem a small criticism, but members of health authorities are busy people. The health practitioners work full time in the health service; the politicians are often councillors and probably hold down outside jobs as well. If they are not reading the papers they get they obviously aren't familiar with the workings of the health authority, so it is small wonder they are always asking for additional information.

Paradoxically, less paper, presented in a more digestible way, will lead to better informed members, and better informed members are much more likely to understand how the managers have arrived at a particular policy, and are therefore more likely to support it. And when they don't, the debate is on key points not the minutiae.

I always find it helpful to think of people owning a strategy. I like to discover how far down an organisation the people who work in it understand and share its aims. In the ideal set-up everyone from the chairman to the doorman shares a common purpose – they all feel they own the strategy. At Shropshire the only people who seem to own the strategy are Frank and Ken and a few top managers. And quite naturally it feels like a mighty burden.

I have sadly some experience of shutting things down and it's almost impossible to achieve unless people believe that the action is inevitable and what you are putting in its place is going to be better. And in Shropshire they don't.

Frank and Ken seem to imagine that the job of a health service manager, or any manager for that matter, is to formulate plans in isolation. Then, thanks to the breathtaking logic of their plans, they expect everyone to go along with them. This approach works if what you propose is uncontroversial. It breaks down as soon as you need to do something more adventurous, when it becomes an absolute necessity to involve as many people as possible in the formulation of policy.

In the context of a district health authority, it means involving the members of the authority, and the medical staff. It is blindingly obvious, but quite simply, the more people who believe in your policy the better the chance of winning over the hearts and minds of the public at large.

I know that my experience of the health service is relatively restricted, but from what I have seen, the most successful districts are those which involve the medical staff in management. Frank agrees, but says doctors only want to get on with their job, and actually want management to free them from the responsibility of having to think about priorities and budgets. I disagree. Bob Wilson, the consultant physician at the Royal Shrewsbury, impressed me with his ability to combine management with doctoring. Frank's view may have been true ten years ago, but I sense that the realities of operating within such tight budgets has kindled doctors' interest in management. And those I met during my time investigating Shropshire all appeared keen to have a greater say.

I hope my time at Shropshire hasn't been wasted. I would like to feel that I have helped Frank and Ken get a handle on what is a vast and complex management problem. I don't underestimate the enormity of their task, but perhaps I have been able to hand them the loose end of wool so that they can begin to unravel the tangle they have got themselves into.

My prescription for Shropshire is straightforward. The authority must simplify procedures, produce plans which are achievable, and involve more people.

I have suggested new ways of presenting information to their members, and although to begin with these worthy men and women may feel cheated if the postman no longer knocks with monthly mountains of paper, I hope they will persevere. In the end I am sure everyone will benefit: the members will understand the problems better, decisions will be made more firmly; and members will be more committed to them.

And the smaller hospitals? I hope the authority has the courage not only to investigate mixed-economy solutions, but, if the sums add up, to go out and sell the idea to the public.

Later on in the year, I learn that Ken Morris had decided

to quit his job as district general manager. I don't know whether the stresses and strains of working for the NHS finally got to him but he is joining a growing band of health service managers who are going over to work in the private sector, where the job of management must at least appear less controversial.

He has been replaced, at least temporarily, by Jim Bartlett who arrives from Mid-Staffordshire District Health Authority with a ferocious reputation for management efficiency. In fact, it's all change at Shropshire. Frank Jones gave up the chairmanship of the health authority in April 1990.

I don't know how much my intervention helped, but I was very pleased when I heard that five of the smaller hospitals – Market Drayton, the Beeches at Ironbridge, Much Wenlock, Bishops Castle and Ellesmere – may stay open as independent hospital trusts.

The authority is now actively exploring the possibility of renting these hospitals at a peppercorn rent to hospital trusts which will operate them independently of the health authority. The authority intends keeping some of its own services going in these hospitals, but in the main they will operate as private nursing homes.

Providing long-stay nursing care for the elderly has traditionally been one of the main functions of the smaller hospitals. The difference now is that the facility, instead of being paid for by the health authority, will now be paid for by the individual, with fees paid by the DSS for those who can't afford it.

6

Churchill Tableware

Churchill is not a household name like Wedgwood or Royal Doulton, but in Stoke-on-Trent, the home of Britain's potteries, everyone knows it as the largest family-run pottery in the business.

The Churchill Group has two principal divisions: it makes china for the hotel industry, and it makes mass-market tableware for the home, including such perennials as the classic blue and white willow pattern. They also have a small factory which makes mugs.

This is the story of the Churchill Group and the three Roper brothers, Michael, Stephen and Andrew, who run it. Each brother has a slightly different outlook, as Andrew explained when I first met him. Andrew has coined nick-names for them all. There is up-market Steve – he wants to move the mass-market tableware into a more expensive price bracket; there is down-market Andy – he is always being accused of selling too cheaply; and there is make-your-mind-up Mick – he has to decide what big items of capital expenditure to make.

The hotelware is extremely profitable, but what worries the brothers is the lack of orders and fading profitability of their mass-market tableware division, which operates out of an entirely separate factory on the edge of Tunstall. They would like to return a profit at least 10 per cent on sales. However, for the last ten years they have never achieved more than 7 per cent and when the figure sank to just 2 per cent in 1989 they thought they would be lucky to break even.

Everyone in Stoke is haunted by memories of the recession that hit the potteries between 1979 and 1981, when sales and profits were squeezed by a combination of high inflation, an overvalued pound and high interest rates. It was a time of redundancies and receiverships which saw many small family firms go out of business for good. As the brothers wonder whether they are facing another recession, the recollection of those two difficult years a decade ago runs like a leitmotiv through their deliberations.

With so much gloom in the air, it is sometimes difficult to remember that the pottery industry is one of Britain's industrial success stories – how I wish there were more. British companies still supply some 80 per cent of the home market for tableware and this is in the face of stiff competition from the Far East and Eastern Europe. They are also some of our most successful exporters. The industry sells abroad over half of what it makes, with factories like Churchill's tableware division actually exporting between 60 and 70 per cent of their production.

The three brothers are still in the process of trying to decide how to improve the tableware factory's prospects and they are hoping I may be able to clarify their thinking. They can't decide how much to cut costs and go for volume at the lower end of the market, and to what extent to introduce more medium-priced ranges where the emphasis is on margin.

The potteries are a close-knit world. The industry is

almost entirely centred on the five Staffordshire towns of Stoke, Burslam, Hanley, Longton and Tunstall, and for many people working anywhere else would be a major wrench. Michael, who has been in the business longest, clearly has a deep affection for the industry. His early designs are now turning up in antique shops, which he says sparks off happy memories of the stories that brought them into being.

The Ropers can trace back the origins of the Churchill Group to Broadhursts, a pottery company started by their grandfather in 1926. The factory closed down during the Second World War, but their father got it going again in 1945 when he came out of the forces.

Michael, the eldest brother, has looked after the production side of the business since he joined the firm in 1959. Stephen joined a year later but, on his own admission, found he wasn't cut out for production management. He moved over to the sales side where he developed the company's export markets.

The youngest brother, Andrew, qualified as an accountant. He spent a few years working for Lotus Shoes before he too joined the family firm. In his early days with the firm he looked after the company's finances, but in recent years he has concentrated on selling.

The figures show the combined results of the tableware and hotelware business. Sales have more than doubled in the six years from 1982 to 1988, and pre-tax profits have increased even faster, from £220 000 to £1.5 million. Profits as a percentage of sales – one measure of a company's efficiency – grew from just over 2.5 per cent in 1982 to a record 6.9 per cent in 1987. Much of this is due to the success of the hotelware business and the first sign that margins in the tableware business were coming under

Financial results for Churchill Tableware
(31 December year end)

	1979	1980	1981	1982	1983
Sales (£m)	5.5	6.0	6.9	8.4	9.8
Pre-tax profits (£000)	151	152	234	220	257
	1984	**1985**	**1986**	**1987**	**1988**
Sales (£m)	11.0	15.6	17.2	20.2	22.5
Pre-tax profits (£000)	267	520	848	1388	1453

pressure came the following year when they slipped back to 6.5 per cent.

Of all the companies I visited for this television series, Churchill is the most professionally managed. It had already done many of the things I have been advocating in the other companies I went to. The company has invested, albeit cautiously, in its factories – it claims its tableware plant is one of the most efficient in the world. And in the last couple of years a new management team has been recruited.

The three Roper brothers spend endless hours chewing over the Churchill cud, but what I was really interested in finding out was whether or not they actually shared a common dream for their company. If they do I found it very difficult to pin down.

Each brother has a different view of the business, and each wants a different degree of involvement. Their views are coloured by their background, expertise and actual daily experience of the factories and their workings. They are trying to find some sort of consensus to take them forward but for all their efforts they are finding it very difficult to come up with any proposals.

Michael is the brother who has spent his life on the production side, and as such he appears the most committed of the three. He is a potter through and through, a passion he has passed on to his son, who has recently started working in the firm. Michael's first instinct is to look after the factories. He is proud of the fact that at Turnstall they have created a mass production factory which, when conditions are right, is efficient enough to take on the low-cost producers of the Far East and Eastern Europe. The trouble is that conditions haven't been right now for the last couple of years, so even Michael is having to change his position.

Michael describes himself as a bit of a Jekyll and Hyde. He now thinks Churchill's drive for volume at the lower end of the market has been at the expense of moving with the market. The company has spent so much time trying to make their tableware cheaper and cheaper and not enough time really trying to find out what people want that they have lost sight of where the market is going.

He now agrees with Stephen that they should be thinking of extending their ranges of tableware into the middle market area, where most of the growth has occurred over the last couple of years. He thinks they should be putting more effort into distribution, marketing and extending their range of customers, but without deserting their mainstream business.

I get the feeling that Stephen would like to reduce the amount of time he spends managing the family business. He feels that maybe they all do too much soul-searching, and that they should be placing more responsibility on the shoulders of their newly appointed managers.

Even though his major concern is with the structure of the company, he is undoubtedly the strongest advocate of moving up-market. But he is under no illusion about the difficulty of this task. It is not simply a question of developing new shapes and increasing the sophistication and amount of surface decoration. There are other worries. For example can a factory with the mass-market culture produce the necessary quality? And new back-up systems will have to be developed to handle a different sort of customer.

Andrew's views, on the other hand, are coloured by his accountancy background, and whatever he does, wherever he goes, there is a big part of him which is always counting the cost. He is acutely aware that this allegedly super-efficient tableware factory is in fact some kind of monster with a monstrous appetite to be fed. He calls it the sausage machine. They are making over 600 000 pieces of crockery a week, and unless that sausage machine keeps on churning them out, costs start to spiral. Making for stock is one solution, but after a while this puts an intolerable strain on cash flow. Some weeks they come into work and there aren't any orders; then everyone just has to knuckle down and pull some in. The need to keep the kiln full and 500 people employed is always at the front of Andrew's mind.

Andrew would also like to know how they can strengthen their corporate identity. Previously the company had operated under a number of different names. There was Broadhurst for domestic tableware, and Bridgwood for hotelware. Five years ago they decided to scrap the old names, some of which were 125 years old, and bring the whole lot under the Churchill banner, which up until then had been used principally on the mugs.

The move has had only limited success. Andrew feels it

has brought the company greater recognition within the trade, but he would like the name to mean something to the City and the public at large and he would like to know how to achieve this without spending a lot of money on advertising. He is much more wary than his brothers about the percentage of the business they move up-market into the middle price range. He is convinced they can't afford to neglect their existing market and that at the same time they should be paying more attention to design.

So what are my first impressions? I have looked at the numbers and the annual reports but I haven't yet visited the tableware factory. The plant plainly isn't making enough money, at least not enough to reinvest and keep the business going over the long term. The temptation to move up-market is obvious but that can be a difficult trick to pull off.

Stephen would like Churchill to go public by 1992 and have its shares quoted on the City's Unlisted Securities Market. To achieve this aim he needs a consistent profit record and the tableware factory really must earn more money.

I am worried by the differences of style, temperament and expectation between the three brothers. Stephen is currently the managing director, but this is really only nominal. In reality there are three managing directors. They all seem to like each other immensely and on their own admission they talk things through in enormous detail to try and arrive at some sort of consensus. In theory this is fine; after all it is a system that works very well in Japan. But here I get the feeling it means that everyone sits on the fence and decisions just don't get made.

They have wisely taken steps to strengthen their management but, instead of stepping back to play a more strategic role, the brothers are still getting bogged down in the minutiae of management. They are not allowing their new managers enough space to show what they are capable of. They aren't putting enough trust in them and they aren't requiring enough of them.

The factory is production led. What is driving the tableware business is the need to keep the kiln full. It is not being driven by the needs of the market place or the customer. As a result factory output is still concentrated at the bottom end of the market.

Promotional work for the likes of petrol companies has become their staple. The attractions of this type of work lie in the huge volumes of a limited range of products. But by their very nature, promotions don't last for ever, so the business is volatile, and you don't always know where the next promotion is coming from.

According to Stephen it was the middle market which was destroyed in the 1979–81 recession. But this sector is now being rebuilt and some highly profitable companies are emerging which seem capable of returning a profit on sales in excess of 14 per cent, the same return Churchill expects to see on its hotelware. Stephen attributes their success to good products and distribution but most importantly, he thinks, to their investment in marketing. He uses the example of these companies to back his argument that the products of the tableware factory should be moved into a more expensive price range.

Churchill's tableware factory has taken the lion's share of the company's investment. In the early 1980s the brothers believed that the more efficient they made the factory, the better chance it had of making a healthy return on sales. That may have been true ten years ago, but it certainly isn't true today.

I don't think you can win any more just by having a

production advantage. You can have a production disadvantage, but that is an entirely different problem. But you can't build a business on the basis that you can churn things out cheaper than anyone else. You must have something else as well. It is important to find a niche, or establish a brand, so you can then push home your competitive advantage. And so far Churchill haven't achieved this.

The visit to the tableware factory is fascinating. To me the potteries still conjure up images straight out of Arnold Bennett of grim, red-brick factories, belching out filthy smoke from hundreds of towering kiln chimneys, all crammed together between rows of back-to-back houses. And there is no doubt that there are still powerful traces of this world in the five towns. But Churchill's tableware factory is not one of them. Situated on the edge of Tunstall, the single-storey modern factory is surrounded by open, green space.

Before my visit, I had been puzzled by something which Andrew had said. I know the pottery industry is labour intensive and that many of the jobs depend on skill and experience which cannot easily be replaced by machines. Still I was surprised when Andrew told me that wage costs at the tableware factory accounted for around 36 per cent of the cost of production. I thought this exceedingly high for a company which claims to have one of the most efficient mass production factories in the country.

This is the first time I have seen a pottery in action. There is a fascination in watching items we take for granted in our daily lives come off the production line in their thousands.

I love the detail and the useless bits of information one picks up, for example the composition of earthenware, which I learn is made up of ball clay mined in Devon and

Dorset, china clay mined in Cornwall and flint, all bound together with the mineral feldspar, imported from Scandinavia.

Eddie Orme, the manufacturing director, takes me round the factory, and what really interests me is to find out how serious they all are about driving down costs.

The factory employs some 375 workers. Remember, this factory claims to be very efficient, so I was genuinely surprised to see just how many jobs which could be mechanised were still being done by hand.

Teapots, bowls and jugs are made in moulds. At Churchill the wet clay is poured into the moulds by hand, and yet there are machines which can tackle the task, even if the inside still has to be finished by hand. Other jobs where there is scope for further mechanisation include the handling of cups, the trimming of handle seams when they emerge from their moulds, and fixing handles to cups. I spot countless tasks around the factory which could either be mechanised or where a simple, cheap robot costing around £6000 could do the job with more accuracy. There are already two machines for taking the seams off the handles and another two are on order, at a cost of £10 500 each, but another four are needed before this particular task is entirely mechanised.

Efficiency is also a function of the number of bits of crockery that must be rejected because they aren't up to standard; the rejection rate is 18 per cent. I think this is far too high, even though I am told it is about average for the industry. The less you handle, the less you risk producing substandard goods, which to my mind is another powerful argument for mechanising as many jobs as possible.

There has been a lot of talk of buying dust-pressing machines which are now being widely used to reduce the cost of making plates in bone china and porcelain factories. Dust pressing (a process which uses clay granules rather than wet clay) can produce significant energy savings but each machine costs £500 000, and to make much impact the factory would need at least two.

I am far from convinced this particular investment makes much sense. For a start no one knows if the technology works with earthenware, and the pay-off in terms of energy and manpower savings would take several years. Robots, on the other hand, pay for themselves in less than a year.

A state of the art, computer-controlled kiln was installed just over three years ago. The kiln's voracious appetite for volume is a big part of the factory's problem. But what it lacks in flexibility it makes up for in efficiency. Most earthenware is fired twice, once before glazing and once after. With this kiln the mugs and the cups need only one firing, although for technical reasons plates still need to be fired twice.

Of all the factories I have visited for this series, this is the one which is most professionally managed, and I was particularly impressed by the quality and commitment of the middle management. But even here I find complacency at the top. I know the pottery industry is labour-intensive, but any factory operating at the mass production end of the market which accepts labour costs of nearly 40 per cent of the cost of production will at some time face a day of reckoning.

Going round the factory, and at a very rough guess, I estimate that cost savings of around £1 million a year could be made by mechanising 100 jobs, and that natural wastage would reduce the need for massive and painful redundancies. This factory is on the investment treadmill.

If it doesn't invest it will become uncompetitive. Quite simply, investment is the cost of staying in business.

Not that everything is doom and gloom. The people who work here, even those with extremely repetitious jobs, seem happy and there is a good atmosphere. I am slightly concerned that they aren't better informed about the business, although I have to say they don't seem to mind.

If Churchill is to shift a proportion of the output of the tableware factory up-market, it will have to become much more marketing oriented, and its whole management philosophy must become less dominated by the need to keep that sausage machine churning out the volume. On the sales side at least the brothers have recognised their weakness. They have recently appointed a new senior marketing man, Bernard Burns, with a solid background in consumer marketing. Before joining Churchill he was with Courtaulds, where he worked on the successful Dorma range of bedlinen. Before that he was with those masters of marketing, Marks & Spencer.

The other component of this shift from being production driven to being market driven, must be design. Churchill has a design team, who are positively buzzing with new ideas. The trouble is there are only two of them, and for the moment at least, I don't feel that their enthusiasm, or the need for better design, is getting through to top management.

Not that Peter Condliffe, Churchill's design development manager, and his assistant designer, Candy Kelsall, actually feel particularly constrained by the fact there are only two of them. Being such a small department they get to do a bit of everything: looking out for market trends, working with outside designers; they even get time to do a bit of designing themselves. This is not to say they don't feel constrained by the management's lack of commitment to design. They both feel the company is going to have to invest much more heavily in this area if they are going to stand a cat in hell's chance of moving up-market.

There are several aspects to the design of pottery which I hadn't appreciated before I met Peter and Candy. The first is that it is extraordinarily cheap to buy in new designs. Apparently a new design for a plate only costs around £150. I can't believe that at such a rate of pay freelance designers can hope to make a living wage. It seems to me astonishing that an industry, whose success depends so heavily on design, should treat its designers with such contempt and I can't believe that one day they won't regret it, when all the designers disappear to Limoges in France or Selbe, the home of West Germany's pottery industry.

Churchill spends around £5000 a year on buying in designs, a figure Peter and Candy think ought to be doubled or even trebled and, as Candy says, they should be flooding the place with design.

Peter and Candy say Churchill won't be able to move into the middle market area until they can introduce more colour into their designs. At the moment the factory is only capable of using two or three colours. But putting in machines capable of processing four or five colours is a major investment for Churchill. One machine costs £78 000, and this factory would need six. They are buying one machine, but this is going into the mug factory.

Candy in particular feels that Churchill needs to make this major investment in design. She thinks the company always follows rather than leads when it comes to putting money into design technology: it never seems to want to be first with any new development. Caution has characterised its attitude, and Candy feels strongly that a big imaginative leap forward is needed.

Bernard Burns, the new marketing man, has a very different perspective on design. Like the good marketing man he is, he doesn't feel you necessarily get a winner just by producing fifty or sixty new designs a year, from which you then choose three or four you just happen to like. According to Bernard the key to finding a winner is extensive consumer testing.

Throughout my visit to Churchill it has been assumed that one of the solutions to the problems of the tableware factory is to start producing more expensive china for the middle range of the market. The company is already taking the first small step in this direction with a new range called Mille Fleurs.

I finally get to see the range when Bernard shows me round the tableware factory's showroom. Miraculously, the design – a dainty floral with a coloured stripe round the edge – is in three colours, even though in theory the factory can only produce two. This is a one-off which, says Bernard, has effectively been achieved by sleight of hand. He readily admits that in the long term they probably wouldn't be able to go up-market without some further investment in colour and design technology.

Mille Fleurs may only be Churchill's toe in the water of the middle market, but it is a breakthrough none the less. For a start, while most of Churchill's boxed sets sell for £19.95, Mille Fleurs will sell at £24.95 or £29.95. And whereas previously new designs have effectively been chosen by the Roper brothers in consultation with the marketing and design departments, Mille Fleurs has been extensively consumer tested, and the reaction has been very favourable.

Bernard's marketing plan for Mille Fleurs and his understanding of how the market, especially at home, is structured, is undoubtedly very impressive. However, I am disappointed to find that none of his plans have been hardened up with rigorous calculations of their effect on margins.

It may be stating the obvious, but the long-term future of this factory depends quite simply on cutting input costs and raising output prices. The factory has to be made more efficient, and ways have to be found to get a higher price for what it sells. Of course, this is easier said than done, but unless the top management actually sees this as their mission in life, the message is unlikely to filter down to the rest of management.

The whole point of moving up-market is to get a better return on sales. So I was shocked to learn that Bernard wasn't expecting the margins to be any higher on Mille Fleurs than on their traditional boxes of crockery.

He was hoping to get the margin by persuading his big customers to stock individual items so that shoppers could add to their collections or replace items that get broken. Here the margins can be as high as 20 per cent: but there is no guarantee that any of the multiples will agree to stock Mille Fleurs on this basis. Nor has Bernard worked out how much extra it would cost the company in higher stocks, smaller production runs, and more expensive distribution.

Keeping your eye on profits is the best business discipline there is, and the future of this factory depends on it. Failure to do so often means you end up pursuing solutions which may be in the right direction but which aren't ambitious enough.

If Mille Fleurs is successful, Bernard expects to sell

around 1.5 million pieces of crockery in the first year. But what effect is this going to have on profits? The answer is – not very much. For a start 1.5 million pieces is only two and a half days' production for the tableware factory. Margins on the boxed sets are no higher than on the traditional lines, and there is no guarantee that multiples will stock individual items where the margins are higher.

However, there is no doubt that Bernard has injected Churchill with some sorely needed marketing expertise. As he says, the company is dominated by its factories and its tableware factory with its appetite for volume, in particular. What the brothers like doing is making pottery, and if at the end of the day they sell it, well, that's an advantage. It seems this is a common problem throughout the industry. The whole culture is production driven and even highly successful companies are obsessed by the need to keep those kilns full.

Bernard is convinced there needs to be a change of philosophy at Churchill. The company must be much more prepared to find out what the customer wants and then look at whether or not it can provide it. But it seems that someone has been warning him off. Apparently the potteries abound with tales of smart-alec outsiders who think they can turn round bankrupt potteries by giving the customers what they want, but who soon depart the scene wiser but poorer, simply because they have failed to understand that making pottery is still an art. Well, that may be true, but I don't think it should stop anyone from keeping their eye firmly on the profits.

It is now the end of a very long day, and Michael, Stephen, Andrew and I meet up again to see if we can extract anything useful from what I have learned during what is, after all, a lightning visit to an industry which before today I knew nothing about.

I agree with them that the principal problem facing the business as a whole is the tableware factory, where the set-up forces them into a position of having to supply the low-margin, high-volume end of the market. That being the case, they must make the factory as efficient as possible. They are very proud of this factory, so they are obviously surprised when I tell them I am convinced that costs could be squeezed by another £1 million a year, by mechanising around 100 unskilled jobs with the introduction of more robots.

But this on its own is not going to be enough to save the factory and give it a future well into the next century. The continual battle on production costs must be coupled with a move up-market.

I explain that it was only during the course of my day at the factory that I had fully understood the problems of moving up-market, and the limitations of the present set-up. There is the disadvantage of only being able to offer two-colour designs, when any effective move up-market will require designs in at least four colours. And there is the size of the design budget. I am shocked to find that a company with sales of more than £20 million was spending only £5000 a year on buying in new design; I agree with Churchill's designers that this needs to be substantially increased.

I don't think Churchill is capable of putting into effect this dual policy of cutting costs and going up-market unless a lot more money is invested in their tableware factory. The three brothers have followed a conservative investment policy which has kept the balance sheet clean of debt. I think the time has now come to depart from this policy.

The figure I mention is £1.5 million, which is the amount I want to see invested in the tableware factory. The £1 million which should be spent on mechanisation will pay for itself within the year. The real gamble is the £500 000 they ought to be spending on bringing in machines capable of producing four-colour designs. This will only pay for itself over a number of years, and only if Churchill's move up-market achieves higher margins.

But there isn't just the tableware factory. The brothers must balance the investment needs of all the businesses within the group. I don't think the tableware factory will survive without fresh investment, but is this throwing good money after bad, and would the company get a better return on its investment if it invested the money somewhere else?

We start to talk about the brothers' roles as shareholders, directors and managers. Stephen would like to step back and distance himself from his purely managerial role. As we have already seen, the company has wisely spent the last two years strengthening its senior and middle management. I think Stephen is right: the brothers should now stop worrying about the bread-and-butter problems of management. The business is now large enough to need a very top layer of management which is concerned with the company's development and long-term strategy and who spend their time setting objectives and then driving everyone very hard to achieve them. I believe this is the role that Michael, Stephen and Andrew should adopt.

Michael and Andrew will find it difficult to let go, but unless they do, and unless they learn to give their senior managers responsibilities and targets which have a bearing on the success of the operation, their very able managers will desert them out of sheer frustration. They must learn to ask their managers for solutions to problems, rather than coming up with their own and asking their managers simply to implement them. I suggest they start by asking Eddie Orme to provide a plan for reducing production costs in the factory by £500 000 a year, and Bernard Burns for a marketing plan aimed at producing a further £1 million of profit within the next two years.

I am convinced the brothers are going to be pleasantly surprised at how well their managers respond to having real responsibility heaped upon them. I hope I am proved right.

Peter Siddall has been the Churchill Group's non-executive chairman for the last four years. A management consultant, he spends just one or two days a month on Churchill business. None the less he has done much to update the company's management methods. It was Peter who suggested the divisional structure, separating the company into three sections: tableware, hotelware and mugs. It is only since this structure has been in force that the brothers have really been able to measure the performance of their various activities. He was also responsible for suggesting the recruitment of a new layer of senior and middle managers to relieve the brothers of the burdens of day-to-day management.

Peter Siddall is based in Barnes, a leafy south London suburb. His offices overlook a boat race stretch of the Thames. Culturally, it couldn't be further from Stoke-on-Trent.

I am extremely interested to have Peter's views on the company he chairs. Non-executive chairmen should remain at one remove from the company and if they are any good they will bring freshness and insight to bear on the company's operations. I want to know if Peter Siddall shares my diagnosis of the company's problems, and how he copes with the differences of temperament and outlook of the three brothers.

We basically agree that for the next couple of years the hotelware business is set fair. He is as concerned as I am about the tableware factory and shares my view that the profit return on sales must be improved, by a two-pronged attack: cutting production costs, and moving up-market and selling more expensive products. The brothers can subscribe to both of these aims, although they seem less convinced of the need for the former. What I find so difficult to understand is the lack of urgency and the lack of concrete plans for achieving these goals.

They are problems on which Peter is able to shed some light. In the small enclosed world of the potteries the Churchill Group is seen as very successful, and Peter is rightly concerned that I shouldn't underestimate the three brothers' achievements. The industry traditionally views itself as highly labour-intensive. And at a time when most of the old crafts are dying out, it is surprising to learn that in the potteries it is the factories which have the largest craft element, and can therefore command the highest prices for their wares, which earn the best margins.

Automation is not part of the deep-rooted culture of the potteries, so any remotely mechanised factory, such as Churchill's tableware operation, is seen as highly advanced. This certainly goes a long way towards explaining why the brothers and I have such divergent views on the potential for further mechanisation in the tableware factory.

Peter thinks this also explains their apparent lack of ambition. They would obviously like to push Churchill on to greater heights, but they are also well satisfied with what they have achieved so far, so there is an element of resting on their laurels. As he says, it is difficult to tell people who have achieved so much that what they are now doing is not good enough and that they must push their business harder.

It is a problem, but not an impossible one to solve. Because they have built their business in a certain way, they are trapped into a particular way of thinking. They need to be convinced that improving the profitability of the tableware factory is achievable and in a relatively short space of time. Then I think they might be able to run a tighter, more focused and more profit motivated operation.

Peter feels as I do, that the size of the company now dictates that the brothers should distance themselves from the daily tasks of management and take on the strategic role of making plans and setting objectives for their managers. He senses that this adjustment will be hard to make. He knows that part of his task is to persuade them to make it and that, if they don't, they risk losing some very capable managers.

On the surface the brothers don't appear very receptive to new ideas. However, the reality is very different. Over the four years that Peter Siddall has been chairman they have accepted and implemented most of his ideas. Yet I do detect an undercurrent – that in some respects Peter feels he is knocking his head against a brick wall. I believe him when he says he is constantly trying to prod and push the brothers into being more ambitious for Churchill, and that somehow the message falls on deaf ears.

So I am surprised and gratified that one of my proposals for a brainstorming session is likely to happen. The brothers are planning to take a group of top managers to a quiet country hotel for a two- or three-day strategic planning session where they can completely escape from the stresses of daily management in order to shift gear and formulate some plans for Churchill's long-term future.

I am now due to meet the brothers for the last time. Since my meeting with Peter Siddall, I am particularly concerned about the management issues confronting the three brothers, and I am determined to winkle out the differences between them, something I have so far singularly failed to do. At Churchill, I am convinced that this is the problem that dare not speak its name. But until these differences are clarified and out in the open, I can't see how these brothers can start speaking with the one voice which is necessary to drive this company in the single-minded way it deserves.

This is not to ignore the problems of the tableware factory. The brothers know they must increase the profits from this factory if it is to survive. They have a strategy to move up-market, I want them to tackle production costs. But I now feel that until these basic management issues are tackled their plans for saving the tableware factory are destined to go off at half cock.

This is why the launch of the first middle-market range, Mille Fleurs, appears so threadbare and tentative. The profit margin looks better since I first talked to Bernard. The price of packaging for the boxed sets, the main way the crockery is sold, has come down, so increasing the profits. But there is a lack of self-confidence about the launch. Churchill sells most of its mass-market crockery in boxes of twenty for £19.95. Instead of moving Mille Fleurs up to a completely new price bracket and charging £29.95, which in terms of design is justified, they have opted for the half-way house of £24.95.

And where are the successors to Mille Fleurs? Any company which is serious about carving out a new niche for itself in the marketplace would already have the next couple of designs waiting in the wings. Here there is no sign of them, although to be fair to Churchill they have asked some Italian designers to come up with ideas.

They are a likeable bunch, these brothers, which is part of the trouble. Because they like and respect each other, they always try to reach a consensus but, as Michael acknowledges, this sometimes means no decision is actually reached. It also leads to a certain diffidence. They are modest about their achievements and would think it rather ungentlemanly to appear too thrusting and ambitious.

This is a company where conflict is kept under lock and key. The atmosphere is stifling. You feel that if only the brothers could have a flaming row it would clear the air, and once they had forgiven each other for any cruel things they had said to each other, they would be able to find a common way forward.

We spend several hours turning over the issues, and just as I am beginning to think the arguments could carry on going round and round in circles for hours, the fog begins to lift, and I begin to get a picture of where each brother stands.

Michael, the eldest, and in many ways the brother to whom the others defer, favours organising the business very much along divisional lines, giving each brother one factory to oversee. Stephen would like the brothers to take on a strategic and planning role, setting objectives for the managers and ensuring that they implement them. Andrew would like them to be driven by the desire to become a public company in three to five years' time, with all that implies for producing steadily rising profits during the intervening years.

These are very real differences, but not so great that they

can't be resolved. I feel they are closer to agreement than disagreement, but until they can all agree to go forward in the same way, the management of Churchill will continue to lack ambition, clarity and precision.

I suggest they get some process help. This means getting together with a professional who has the skills to help groups of individuals within companies resolve their differences. Every board I have been on has, at some point, needed some process help, and I have always found it useful. Their job is not to offer advice or easy solutions. Their skill is uncovering the problem and providing a framework in which individuals who have to operate in groups can say what they feel. This can sometimes be an uncomfortable business, but in my experience it is often the best way to start unlocking the differences between managers which are preventing them from moving forward with a common view and shared aims.

I left Churchill feeling a little dispirited. Peter Siddall often ends up with the impression that much of what he says slips like water off a duck's back, and I now know how he feels.

What I hadn't fully appreciated is that none of the three brothers is particularly outgoing. It is not their style to jump up and down and shout 'Eureka!', which of course is what everyone going in to advise companies wants to hear. Quite rightly they are suspicious of instant solutions; they like to take time to consider and ponder. So I was particularly pleased to learn, some weeks later, that much of what I had been saying had quietly been taken on board, and that the reaction was so far very positive.

Now that more is being asked of them, Eddie Orme and Bernard Burns are both showing their true capabilities.

Their enthusiasm is filtering down to middle management and this is giving the place a much greater sense of urgency.

Eddie's cost-saving plan for the tableware factory is being dealt with constructively. The board has agreed to spend £33 000 on three more automatic handling machines. These are robots which transfer pieces of pottery from the forming machine on to a conveyor belt. And they will spend another £42 000 during 1990 on four more machines for removing handle seams, thus completing the automation of this process. I can only hope this is the beginning of a major new investment programme.

Bernard Burns says I have had an effect on the way the brothers hand down instructions. Instead of just telling their managers what to do, they are now setting them targets – they have been told to find ways of getting the tableware factory to produce a 10 per cent profit margin – and it is up to them how they achieve them. These days Bernard can't wait to get to work in the morning because for the first time he feels he is being allowed to do the job he was hired to do.

Bernard thinks I failed to unite the brothers behind a common cause, although he does feel I raised the tempo and that the whole debate about the future of the tableware operation is now much more lively.

I would still like to see the brothers try and sort out their differences and I regret I haven't been able to persuade them to seek some professional help in this area. Instead they opt for a brainstorming session. In January, the three brothers, chairman Peter Siddall, Churchill's top managers and a couple of outside marketing consultants hole themselves up for two days at Hanchurch Manor, a small hotel in a converted Elizabethan manor house on the edge of the

Potteries. The aim is to produce a marketing plan which everyone in the company is aware of and can work towards.

I am genuinely thrilled to find the brothers are saying there has been something of a sea-change in their management style. Hiring marketing consultants and taking them and senior management away for two days is an entirely new departure. I think they see that their company now requires a higher degree of professionalism and that it must know much more about its customers. The days of running the Churchill Group as a hobby are over.

As their marketing session ends, Michael remarks that since my visit he realises no business can afford to let up, and if the top people do want to step back they must be sure the next layer of management is there driving the business forward. I really know the message has got through when Michael says they must start looking critically at their successful hotelware operation. He is right. I concentrated on the tableware factory because this is where the immediate problems lay, but good managers should be constantly reviewing all their operations, not just those in crisis.

Epilogue

So, at the end of the series, what lessons, impressions and conclusions have I reached?

Firstly, I must recall, with some considerable surprise, that the series proved possible at all. I was not convinced that people and companies would be prepared to open up in the way that they did, or expose themselves in public to advice, much of which was not necessarily what they expected, or in some cases even wanted. I pay every tribute to them. Of course there were concerns about commercial confidentiality because there are always many things about a company's operations, aims and problems which could be of considerable value to a competitor. In the event this did not prove to be a problem – perhaps because I was as frightened of causing harm as they were eager to avoid it. After all, one of my objectives was to try to help the companies concerned (all were well worth helping) and the last thing I wanted was to harm their competitive position.

I also expected that individuals would either 'play to the camera' or be struck dumb by its presence. It would be untrue to claim that everyone forgot the camera's existence – there is no doubt that it is an inhibiting factor for most people – but as soon as we got into the real problems the camera seemed to go away. Everyone I met was really involved and interested in their businesses and what was going to happen to them. This may have been displayed in different ways, but I met no one at any level in any of the companies who was indifferent or uncaring. That is a very far cry from the popular picture of these sorts of business: where the boss is depicted as being interested only in the expense account and living it up, or the troops are portrayed as a bunch of layabouts only waiting for clocking-off timc. Not all the jobs were romantic and yet, at least while we were around, people were involved, concerned and really trying hard. They wanted their companies to prosper and things to be better, so that they could prosper with them. Moreover, in general most of the people I met were capable of doing bigger jobs, and they all had views about how things could be done more effectively. These companies have a mass of potential talent down the line which I am sure would blossom if people were given more responsibility and direction. Most of my experience has been with large companies, and while even the largest is, in reality, a collection of small ones, I still had my stereotypes and expectations of what I was to find and how relevant my ideas might be.

In the event, the differences seemed to me to arise not so much out of relative size as from the different environment in which publicly quoted and privately held companies operate. Over the years I have been so accustomed to trying to respond to the needs of my shareholders, no matter how expressed, while simultaneously trying to safeguard the interests of my fellow employees and our customers, that I had automatically assumed that privately controlled companies would feel the same sort of pressures. It seemed to me that while all of them did feel pressure to improve their performance, the extent of the pressure and the ways in which it was felt were far different to my own experience. It is certainly true that private companies can often take a longer-term view of their affairs than can the public company, which is constantly watching its share price and the analysts' reactions to its strategies. It is equally true that in all the companies I met there was nothing like the remorseless drive to cut costs every year, trying to improve the margins in order to stay continuously ahead of the competition. The view that their job was, day on day, month on month, continually to produce more or better for less was strikingly absent. This led to a diffidence in pricing which was in many cases inexplicable to me. Price is not a function of cost. It is related entirely to what the market will pay, year on year, and what will preserve a company's competitive position. Morgan, for example, considered that its customers who were able to sell their place on the waiting list, or to obtain an immediate profit on their newly delivered car, were in effect 'not very nice people'. The company was quite unwilling to take the point that it could have put the price up itself, making more profit which in turn could be reinvested in more modern equipment. In most cases the sales people were so concerned with moving the volume of the production that they were unwilling even to risk trying a price rise, even though it seemed unlikely that Morgan would actually lose its competitive position by doing so. It is this constant need to test the market, coupled with a clear strategy and knowledge of the competition, that separates the professional salesman from the unprofessional. In the same vein the price that could be obtained was all too often not seen as the benchmark below which the cost had to be pushed. Tri-ang found that it could not obtain the price needed to cover the cost of its garden furniture despite being a company which certainly counted the pennies. Tri-ang worked hard on the more obvious aspects of costs, but was unable to reduce them to the level where the company could make a profit.

This relationship between cost and prices, where both ends of the equation have to be worked on to sustain profit, did not ring as clearly as I expected. I was particularly surprised at this since all the companies, except the health authority, were relatively small, and the leaders of all of them were very close to their customers, their shopfloor and their production teams. Apricot, for example, persisted in adding extra 'goodies' to their computers, all of which added to their cost, despite the conviction of their sales people that they had to undercut the competition in price. They were, therefore, trying to fight with both higher costs and lower prices, in a market where competition is notoriously tough. The building in of avoidable costs to enhance the attractiveness of the product was a perfectly viable strategy, provided the price to Apricot's customers reflected the superiority of the product. In their case Apricot was getting the worst of both worlds. Moreover, sales people will never get a higher price unless they are encouraged, and believe they can outsell the competitors. Once they are convinced they can only do this by cutting prices the business is in trouble, unless the production people can simultaneously cut their costs even faster. The interrelationship of prices and costs was often seen as a 'purely financial matter' rather than actually the entire *raison d'être* of the company. In turn this was because many of the managers saw pure survival as a goal in itself.

Plainly it would be silly to deride the wish to survive. In a number of cases the entire family wealth was tied up in the business. Its preservation was therefore a clear and understandable priority. But the difficulty with this as a way of running a company is that there is never an option to stay still. Unless you are continuously improving your product, reducing your costs and outselling your competitors they will do it to you, and eventually your business will fold. While every person I met acknowledged this as a philosophy, a number of them did not believe it strongly enough to be willing to take the risks which are always associated with change. The downside of the risk seemed more frightening than the upside of the chance of achieving a clear and sustained leadership in their field. The attitudes to change varied enormously, bearing in mind that all of these companies had allegedly invited me in to help them with problems which they foresaw as threatening to their well-being.

The Roper brothers at Churchill, the pottery company, were outstanding in their openness and willingness to consider anything – no matter how outlandish it might seem. Moreover, in their case they were not subjected to irresistible external pressures. Their company was well founded, they had already bought in professional managers, they had ideas about where they wanted to go, and how they were going to get there, and yet in the end they adopted suggestions and ideas with enthusiasm. In some of the other companies external events added to the pressure for change, and resulted in actions which would probably not have occurred without such stimuli. In only one case would I consider that my input was almost totally wasted, and even there there is a chance, albeit slim, that things may begin to shift. Enthusiasm for change is almost non-British, and is in any event the rarest of qualities. It is always easier and safer to stay on the ground we know than to move into the unknown, but the difficulty is that the world around us does not stay still. Experience seems to me to show that organisations and groups of people either change of their own will, on their own terms and under their own control or – alas – events force change upon them. Looked at in this way it is always easier to carry out the operation yourself than lose control and be forced into action by others.

I admired the willingness and enthusiasm of these companies at least to invite an outsider to look at them, and admired the very fundamental changes undertaken by, for example, Copella and Apricot. In all these episodes it has to be remembered that my contribution was only one of many bearing in on each company. In the case of Tri-ang there were active shareholders. In Copella there were the attractions of a different future being offered by the Taunton Cider Company. Apricot's board and external directors were, I am sure, not sitting idly by – and so on. At best the programmes could only have been catalytic in their effect, and yet it was surprising how often the germ of an idea was picked up and spread.

One area of omission which surprised me was the general lack of interest in professionalism. In two of the family businesses care had been taken to ensure that members of the family had studied appropriate subjects and had the basic skills necessary to run a business. Nevertheless, there was no visible feeling that further courses of study would be useful and there seemed even less enthusiasm for training those below the top levels. This affords a frightening comparison with our overseas competitors. They not only recruit young people with a far higher level of pre-employment functional training, but also consistently apply themselves to honing and developing the skills and potential of their people. I suppose it is an attitude of mind, and I have been lucky enough to belong to a company which puts a high premium on training its people continuously. Even now, in retirement, I still pursue the acquisition of new skills on a continual basis. It is surprising that, although people were prepared to look ahead and try to prepare for the future, in practically every case there was very little emphasis on developing the professional skills of employees at every level. There is no company or organisation that I visited that would not have benefited enormously from quite a small diversion of time and money in this way. Too often training is thought of in terms of months of study at a business school, while in reality great results can be achieved from day release, evening classes, distance learning facilities and even specially tailored one- or two-day courses for the company concerned. After all, we spend most of our adult lives at work – it seems unbelievably unambitious to fail to try to improve our abilities. There is no way that untrained amateurs can beat the trained and practised professionals we are up against in Europe and Japan, and we badly need to learn this lesson.

One striking characteristic of the companies was that there was often a lack of clear vision of where they were going. Even when the leaders had such a picture in their minds, as in the case of Tri-ang and Apricot, often they had not been successful in transmitting their vision down the line. While everyone was busy (there was little or no sign of anyone metaphorically leaning on their shovel) there was a curious lack of a feeling of direction and pressure for results. In neither Apricot nor Tri-ang, where the CEOs had possibly over-ambitious aims for their company, could I find the resultant expectations passed on to individual managers or departments. It was almost as though the expectation was that everyone would adjust and know automatically what was expected of them. This might have been possible if the CEOs' dream was shared by the others, but alas that was not the case. This lack of specificity applied to other companies as well. Even Morgan's target of one more car per week did not seem to be broken down into the specific changes needed by each person. It therefore ended in a wrangle over what it meant to whom. People work best when they know exactly what is expected of them, and when that is just a little more than they themselves think they can achieve. This releases energy and poses a challenge, which engenders a real sense of achievement. The Morgan workers simply do not want to make another car a week. From their point of view it doesn't make much difference either to the company or to themselves and, until they do believe in it, it just will not happen. It is this task of creating an exciting and believable vision that fires everyone up. The job of top management is to allocate the responsibility for their contribution to the achievement of the whole to each part of the outfit, without telling them specifically how to carry it out. In really good companies it is a way of life, but in almost all of the companies in this series this sort of approach to business was missing. As a result the business performed less well than it could have done.

The exception to almost all these generalisations was the Shropshire Health Authority, which felt it could do relatively little to improve its lot either by raising prices or by selling more of its services. In fact the solution to its problems seems to me to lie very much in that direction. It must realise its assets, which will generate capital. It has to attract more revenue by, for example, turning the smaller hospitals into trusts which I am pleased to see they are now investigating, and so on. There were plenty of ideas around, but a lack of belief that the management could actually carry out the ideas that were being pressed upon them by their staff. The task of reducing costs by 2–3 per cent per annum should be within any outfit's grasp, but to achieve it management must have the headroom and freedom to operate which should always accompany heavy responsibility. In this management problem I have every sympathy with the hospital administrators, who must feel very lonely. They must feel that they are the jam in the sandwich, that practically everyone can say no to them, while it is almost impossible to find a single person who, on his own, can say yes.

The lesson here seems to me to be that the best strategy is one which can actually be carried out! It is not a bit of good having a plan if there is no practicable way in which resistance to the concept can be overcome. Moreover, it is not much good looking back from where you are and trying to apportion blame. The task and the problem for Shropshire is to find a way of moving ahead, accepting that heavy costs are incurred in the new hospital at Telford. This is a classical case where a complex problem can only be solved by simplifying it. It was not, in my view, an accident that the committee seized with relief on a 'single sheet of paper' solution. It was within everyone's grasp and understanding, and was owned by the entire committee. It also avoided for another year the continuing closure of the smaller hospital which, together with the size and duration of the waiting list, were the sources of so much resistance. I have sympathy with the fact that people find it hard to accept that you can simultaneously reduce the number of hospital beds available, and the waiting list for them. The Council representatives on the committee reflect the feelings of their constituents and the strategy grinds to a halt. In addition to all the other management skills needed by any executive, the manager of a National Health Service district needs to be especially sensitive and politically aware, for in order to succeed he has to carry all the different constituents with him. As well as having the support of the medical profession it is vital that he has the support, or at minimum not the opposition, of the public and the political parties represented on his controlling committee. Every businessman is well aware of the problems of balancing the often conflicting demands of the shareholders, employees, customers and inhabitants of the areas in which they operate. The balancing of such demands is, for all of us, a necessary management skill. For a businessman, however, the opposition of one of these groups may lead to difficulty but is unlikely to stop him stone cold dead in the water. It is this sort of structural difficulty which made the health management task such a fascinating and frustrating one. It is so much easier to suggest helpful management moves than actually to introduce them. Of course the irony is that the health service needs the very highest level of dedicated management skills. Unfortunately it expects to get them for rewards which are financially, and in the terms of job satisfaction and freedom of action, far inferior to those obtainable in the private sector.

The companies I visited taught me a lot. It is all too easy, when anyone suggests improvements or changes, to assume that those doing the job have in some way failed. This is a very common attitude and is yet another reason why British people dislike change. Moreover, this attitude is thoroughly unhelpful to the process of change. In any event there is always a different way, and possibly a better one, to tackle anything in life.

We should applaud the fact that these businesses exist. They make products that people want, they give employment, they pay taxes *and* they contribute to the wealth creation on which all of us depend for our standard of living. We should be grateful that they were willing to allow us all to look into their worlds, in the hope that we would learn a bit more about the reality of business, and in turn they might pick up a few tips about how to do things better. As long as our businessmen and women are constantly striving for improvement and change we should consider ourselves fortunate as a country.

Lastly, and above everything else, I have always believed that business is about people. Of course it is about money and making money but that is the way in which success and failure are measured. The realities of business and its problems are the realities of people in their infinite variety. So it is on their qualities, their courage and drive, their imagination and determination, their weaknesses as well as their strengths, their abilities to work with others and to harness human endeavour and creativity in order to make things that we all need, that business depends.

If the series and this book help to show that business is a human concern and has all the fascination and excitement that our other human activities engender, then it will have served a very worthwhile purpose. I for one wish the companies that took part in the programmes every success for the future. It is in all our interests that they should continue to succeed.

Index

INDEX